Praise for
Shooting Creek and Other Stories

"This excellent collection transcends any genre label. Ultimately, these stories are mysteries of the human heart's darkest regions. Scott Sanders is the real deal and deserves a wide and appreciative readership."

—Ron Rash, *The New York Times* bestselling
author and winner of the Frank O'Connor
International Short Story Award

"Each story is a gem in this dark, atmospheric, treasure box of a collection. Scott Loring Sanders digs deep and peers unflinching into the frail, twisted human heart, revealing its many facets and glittering truths. A stellar collection!"

—Lisa Unger, *The New York Times* bestselling
author of *The Red Hunter*

"These are stories that will keep you up late reading and thinking, stories that mute the concerns of the everyday world while turning up the volume on thrills and excitement. If you're looking for something good to read, this is the book you want."

—Ed Falco, *The New York Times* bestselling
author or *The Family Corleone*

"Sanders's stories are always rich in atmosphere, and his characters are often presented with difficult moral dilemmas. He's an author who prefers a degree of ambiguity to an easy resolution, and that makes his work thought-provoking, as well as unpredictable. Readers in search of well-written, complex suspense tales won't go wrong with a Sanders collection!"

—Janet Hutchings, Editor-in-Chief,
Ellery Queen's Mystery Magazine

SHOOTING CREEK
AND
OTHER STORIES

ALSO BY SCOTT LORING SANDERS

The Hanging Woods
Gray Baby

SCOTT LORING SANDERS

SHOOTING CREEK
AND
OTHER STORIES

Down & Out Books
3959 Van Dyke Rd, Ste. 265
Lutz, FL 33558
www.DownAndOutBooks.com

Cover photo by Mason Sanders
Cover design by Danielle Buynak

ISBN: 1-943402-60-4
ISBN-13: 978-1-943402-60-1

For my sister, Laura

CONTENTS

Frank's Beach

Of all the things I'd discovered over the years, the strangest was a glass eye. When the detector beeped and I plunged my scoop into the sand, I expected the usual spare change. Sure enough, I plucked out a quarter, but then, as the grit sifted through, a fat brown eyeball lingered in my sieve. Heavier than I would've imagined, it was actual glass, not epoxy or rubber or whatever a fake eye is made of these days. What amazed me most was how it had managed—after tumbling in the surf, for years possibly—to stay intact. As it sat in my palm, I poked at it a little, rolled it around with my finger, checking for cracks. Scrutinizing it. Once the sun caught the iris, I determined it Lord God flawless.

And then the questions formed. Who was the owner? How do you purchase a glass eye? Is there a glass eye store, or do you buy online? Do you keep spares in the medicine cabinet like extra bars of soap? And how do you lose one in the first place? Does a massive wave hit you broadside, causing the eye to shoot out at high velocity like a champagne cork? I pictured the eyeball's owner clambering from the rough surf as little boys sat in the sand building castles. They looked up to see a man's face punctured by a gaping hole so horrific that it immediately sent them running for their mommies.

It had been a decade since that discovery, and I'd yet to find anything weirder. I was familiar, of course, with the famous metal detecting stories. A box filled with 16th century coins in Massachusetts, a cache of silver in the Keys from a wrecked Spanish galleon. But for me, my finds were generally the same old thing: spare change, earrings or other jewelry, once a TAG Heuer—though, really, who wore a watch anymore?

I often pondered Blackbeard's buried treasure while scavenging Topsail Island, a narrow spit off North Carolina's mainland. Topsail (pronounced Top-*sull*, from when pirates ransacked the area and used the island as a hideout) wasn't as well-known as Kitty Hawk or Cape Hatteras. And that was fine by me. Tourists kept things busy in summer, but only a handful of us locals remained year-round. I'd lived in my one-bedroom bungalow for over two decades, doing my own hiding out, avoiding the ambush, as it were, of modern-day pirates. Except my pursuers didn't have eye-patches or swords. Instead, they wore custom suits, slick shirts, and gold chains. A car heist had gone seven different shades of wrong when I'd been young, stupid, and living in Jersey. Even twenty-five years later, it wasn't too far-fetched to believe a couple of dudes short on brains but long on memory might suddenly appear, wanting to puncture my skull with ice picks.

I didn't think about it every day, just found it wise to

never fully forget. Like occasionally noticing an old scar on your arm from a schoolyard knife fight—a reminder of how fast things can change if you stop paying attention.

Which gets me to what happened last week. I'd been working flotsam near the dunes after the previous night's hurricane. A glancing blow really, downgraded to a weak Category 1 by the time it made landfall. Ample flooding temporarily closed the main road, the blacktop eaten away by surge. Minor house damage, shingles scattered like confetti, sea grass and skate sacs caught in pilings, on driveways, between deck railings and balconies. An inconvenience for most. An opportunity for me.

I'd set out at sunrise, the morning clear but windy. Sharp gusts repeatedly hiked my shirt up over my paunch, the skin taut as a pale water balloon. Usually I forgot I even had a gut, imagining myself as that bygone twentyish-something athlete instead of the fiftyish-something old man who'd consumed too many beers and fried shrimp platters.

I fought the wind and sparked a cigarette, which, admittedly, didn't help my cause, but hell, we've all got our demons. Currently, I was less worried about my health and more concerned about making rent. I ran the register at the EZ Mart, but in the slow months Mr. Parikh cut back my hours, so digging up loose change or the occasional trinket supplemented my off-season income. Whatever I found, I sold to my buddy Tommy, who ran a pawnshop on the mainland.

When the detector beeped, indicating precious metal, I

dug only six inches before my scoop hit something large and solid. I ditched the sieve and used my hands, digging with gusto, only to retreat with a wince when my pinky got pierced. "Goddamnit," I yelped as blood trickled. It was barely a scratch, minor really, hopefully just from a crab claw or oyster shell fragment. Worst case: a rusty hook or nail. I hadn't had a tetanus shot in forty years. Hadn't seen a doctor in thirty, mainly because I couldn't chance filling out forms, all that info going into some internet database. Not if I wanted to avoid being tossed into the ocean, a manhole cover chained to my ankles— or whatever sick shit those Jersey bastards might devise if I popped back up on the grid.

I sucked at the cut and spat before continuing, brushing more gingerly. Then I discovered what had set the detector off: a ring, gold with a ginormous diamond, five smaller ones inlaid around it like a star. But I had one little problem. A monster fucking problem, if truth be told, that set my heart to rabbit-thumping. The ring was attached to a finger. A whole hand, actually, each nail perfect and painted pink except the index, which was broken, jagged, and smeared with a dot of fresh blood. My blood.

I scanned my surroundings. Other than a scattering of sandpipers and gulls, the beach was abandoned. Waves churned, the sea angry and hungover. I swept a bit more. The hand was delicate, well cared for. I pictured an at-tracttive woman, probably early forties. An odd thought, I admit, imagining a dead woman as good-looking, not to mention a rigid hand was my only barometer for gauging her level of hotness. I had an urge to dig her up and save her, perhaps administer mouth-to-mouth. But I quickly gathered my wits.

I removed more sand, carefully, so as not to injure her. Another weird impulse, yet I felt obliged to show some hint of respect. The hand connected to an arm, and beneath it, scrunched legs in white pants. I glanced around again. Tall dune grass—clustered on the sandy hills, swaying like wheat—shielded me from the road. Bits of sand whipped at my exposed ankles, stinging my skin. A tattered Tar Heels flag flew from an unoccupied oceanfront rental, snapping in the wind. The beach was desolate.

I wasn't sure if I should continue. I'd seen a few stiffs in my day, and I knew that a dead face might cause me to puke-up far quicker than a hand ever could. Or an arm. Or legs in white pants. Dry pants, by the way, which I found peculiar. If the ocean had spit her out during the storm, she would've been soaked. If intentionally buried, last night's downpour would've drenched her. But she was dry. Her disposal, then, had been recent. Very recent. Like only hours-ago-recent. I continued to scrape. An elbow. Lightweight blouse (silk maybe?). A shoulder, locks of hair (brunette, also dry). Throat stained purple with bruises like waxy splashes from a candle.

Beach still empty. Desperate for cigarette. Trawler on horizon, slowly chugging. Had to see that face now. Didn't want to, yet absolutely had to. Beyond her throat, sharp chin melted into painted lips, high cheekbones rouged. One visible earlobe with a diamond stud. Nostrils caked with sand. Eyes closed, thank God, powdered with faint blue shadow. Her temple, where it met the hairline was...was punctured. A black stream, hard and crusty, slipped into her hair above the ear. Flesh puckered and shredded at wound. At entry point.

More than I needed to see.

I covered her face frantically, grabbing at sand, then backtracked: concealed the neck, shoulder, elbow, until I reached that original hand.

Ogled the ring. That fat diamond.

The ripped flag snapped. The trawler chugged. The sandpipers skipped, their tracks dissolving in wet sand like a beautiful mystery. Still no person in sight. I grasped the dead hand, pried and squeezed, tried to slip that ring over her swollen finger. Kept twisting and turning. Once off and safely in my pocket, I considered nicking those matching earrings. Instead, I bolted for home.

At the house, I stared at that ring for hours. Estimated its worth at twenty grand. Considered the woman, somebody's wife or mother. Intentionally buried before sunrise. Not an overboard passenger or drowner. Not an accident.

I couldn't help but think about Trisha, my ex of twenty-five years. We'd dated some in high school, broke up, graduated. With both of us suffocating in our one-traffic-light, one-pizza-place, one-employer (a slaughterhouse), no-grocery-but-four-bars hometown, we reconnected. Occasionally bumped into each other while out drinking, and before I knew it, we got married. There'd never been any real love between us but never any hate or bitterness either. We toughed it out for five years, realized marriage wasn't our thing, split with no hard feelings. Neither of us had any money, any possessions, so there was no messy *this is yours, this is mine.* I stayed in the apartment, she moved to Hawaii on a lark after saving for a ticket. Left with just one suitcase. I hadn't seen her since. Not in person anyway.

A few years ago, I'm watching *Dog the Bounty Hunter*, drinking some cold ones, when Trisha appears onscreen. I about pissed myself, got this weird tingly feeling in my brain like I'd snorted something wicked. She's on the porch of a run-down shack—chickens and garbage and debris strewn across the yard—shrieking at Dog and his posse. Going off, the way I'd seen her do back in the day, usually after a bartender denied her last call. This time she's going ape-shit because Dog had just tackled her boyfriend, then cuffed-and-stuffed him. That dude's in Dog's truck, all bloody above his eye, shirtless and wiry and tattooed, yelling, "Trisha! Baby, I love you. Trisha!" And Beth, Dog's wife, she's restraining Trisha as Trisha strangles the hell out of that porch railing, her neck tendons taut. "Let him go, you asshole," she screams. Of course that was bleeped-out, but I could read those lips, knew them as well as anybody.

Despite her anger, Trisha still looked pretty damned

7

good. Tan, long blonde hair, thin frame in a white tank-top. She'd clearly had a boob job, and her complexion was a bit rough, splotchy like she'd spent some years snorting blow off the sinks of roadhouse bathrooms. But still, you could tell she'd been good-looking once, back before all the hard living drained the pretty out of her. It was strange, surreal I guess, seeing that woman who I'd once known. The two of us so innocent back then, unable to predict what kind of shit-storm Life planned to throw our way.

What had struck me most was how passionate she'd been as she fought off Dog's wife. Normal viewers might've pegged her as just another hysterical drunk or junkie, whacked out of her head. But I saw it differently. She obviously loved that dude, the agony on her face pure and real. At the episode's conclusion, a follow-up paragraph stated her boyfriend escaped two weeks later, only to be shot and killed by the cops. I raised my beer before the TV and said, "Good luck, girl." She'd been cool, maybe a little bat-shit but that didn't mean she didn't deserve happiness, same as the rest of us.

Which brought me back to my own problems: namely that dead woman on the beach and her wedding ring in my house. I'd stashed it in the cigar box with my other strange finds, glass eye included. So who killed her? Who was she? When I tried to envision that face I'd seen earlier, all I got was this funky, lava-lamp-type-shit swirling around, her features warpy and distorted. And then it all melded into this weird-ass version of Trisha— the young Trisha, not the older one I'd seen on *Dog*—

8

except all her teeth were shattered, and the skin of her throat pulsed in a perfect rhythm as if she'd swallowed a beating heart.

On the late local news, a prominent contractor announced his wife was missing. I didn't know the prick personally, but I sure knew *of* him. Sheldon Blackwater, a developer of oceanfront properties and a big opponent of the *Topsail Turtle Project*, something I'd gotten involved with—completely by accident—years ago. I'd been combing the beach when I found a baby logger-head, its flipper missing, struggling as merciless gulls attacked its bloody wound. I scooped up the little guy, took him to the island's turtle rescue facility and, man, I got hooked. Visited every day until he was released six months later. For some folks it's puppies or kittens, for me it was baby turtles.

Sheldon Blackwater had scratches on his face, claimed he and his wife had gotten thrashed in the storm. News footage showed his battered Hummer—hood dented, windshield busted—supposedly from a snapped tele-phone pole. Said he'd run for help and when he returned she was gone. I didn't buy it.

When a photo of his wife, Adrienne, appeared onscreen, I nearly gagged on a bite of Stouffer's lasagna. Because it was her, the dead woman. She lacked the sand and contorted limbs and the hole in the head, but it was her. I wanted to ruin that Sheldon bastard, but unfor-tunately I couldn't call the cops, anonymous or straight-up. Because I had a problem. Specifically, his dead wife's fingernail. Back in Jersey, my DNA and fingerprints were on file, though when the cops collected my blood sample, nobody'd even heard of DNA. They hadn't wanted me or my cousin Mickey anyway; we were small potatoes. They wanted my boss, the guy who ran the chop shop; the guy who paid cash for the hot cars we brought in. And they got him, thanks to me and Mickey pinning two murders on him.

The day after we'd framed the boss-man, the cops found Mickey face-down and naked—save for a pair of tube socks—in the South Branch of the Raritan. It didn't take an Einstein to figure out I was next in line for a swim, so I bolted. Now, because of Adrienne Blackwater's blood-stained finger, trouble was brewing for me once again.

I wasn't overly handy, but I had a basic toolbox, including a hacksaw and a three-pack of blades. I didn't think I'd need more than one, but hell, I'd never tried to saw through human bone before. I figured I'd just remove her pointer but then recalled how I'd pried that diamond off her ring finger. Might be better, then, to cut at the wrist, just take the whole damn hand, launch it into the ocean. I wasn't looking forward to the task, but she'd be discovered one way or another, and, realistically, all the scrubbing in the world wouldn't rid her of my DNA.

Most people knew me, local cops included, and wouldn't think twice if they saw me combing the beach after midnight; a metal detector doesn't care if it's dark.

But a dude walking along with just a hacksaw? That might raise suspicion. So I stuffed it in a backpack and brought the detector along.

I planned to approach from the road, then use the public access boardwalk to shoot in a block shy of her body. But when I got to the steps and headed down the walkway, red and blue flashes spackled the sky. I'd made it halfway when a cop appeared. "You need to turn around, buddy," he said, his Maglite clicking on, blinding me.

"What the hell?" I said, shielding my eyes.

"That you, Frank?" he said.

"Yeah, it's me. Who's that?"

"Officer Reynolds. Sorry, but I can't let you down there."

"What's going on, Craig? And can you cut the damn high beams?" I knew Craig from the EZ Stop. Young kid. He'd come in and shoot the shit, drink free coffee during shifts. He was a good dude, far as cops go.

"I ain't allowed to say," he said, turning off his Maglite, but I sensed an eagerness to spill the beans.

"You busting up a kegger?"

"No, hardly."

"What's with all the lights then?"

"I can't really talk about it, Frank."

"Hell, who am I gonna tell?"

He glanced toward the beach as if expecting his superior. "You heard about that missing lady?" he whispered. "Sheldon Blackwater's wife?"

"Yeah, saw it on the tube."

11

"Pretty sure we found her. Dead. A guy's walking his dog earlier when Fido smells something, runs toward the dunes, starts digging. The guy just called, shitting peach pits."

That one jagged fingernail smeared with a pinch of my blood. No bigger than a chocolate chip or a tab of acid. That's all it would take to lock me up for life.

"Jesus," I said.

"I know, right? Goddamned exciting, huh?"

"Yeah, Craig. Pretty exciting." If my DNA matched up in the national database, which it inevitably would, the local cops wouldn't recognize my given name. But once they saw the accompanying mug shots from back in Jersey? Sure I was older, fatter, balder, but they'd figure it out.

On the morning news, Sheldon Blackwater sat in front of a bouquet of microphones. He wore a suit and tie, hair combed back, graying at the temples. The scratches weren't as noticeable now, makeup I figured. He was probably my age but could've passed for early forties, fit and broad-shouldered. His eyes teared as he discussed how he'd lost his "true love." How he was offering a hundred grand for information leading to an arrest of "the monster." He was so good, so believable, even I almost bought his bullshit.

My one encounter with the man had been at a *Topsail Turtle Project* meeting. He'd actually had the balls to walk in and say he planned to gobble up the beachfront on the south tip of the island, turtle sanctuaries be damned. He'd already uglied North Topsail with giant houses and condos. Now he had his sights set on my little section of beach—Frank's Beach, as many of the volunteers called it. Early in the *Turtle* campaign, when divvying up patrol areas, Karen, our founder, pointed to the map and said, "Obviously this section's Frank's beach since he walks it every day." It had stuck, and I must admit I was proud of the title and that one mile stretch. I did in fact think of it as *my* beach, those little turtle hatchlings as *my* children.

I was a volunteer spotter, a monitor of nests. In the spring, mama loggerheads waddled up on shore, all two, three, four hundred pounds of them. With their flippers, they dug holes near the dunes. Mama laid a hundred-plus eggs, covered them, then slipped back into the ocean, not knowing if her babies would survive. Few did. Rough numbers estimated one out of a hatch might reach adulthood. So volunteers stepped in to boost the odds. During the spring, while metal detecting, I watched for deep trenches in the sand evolving from the surf, resembling tank tracks. The weight of those mama turtles created an X-marks-the-spot trail to nesting sites. They laid at night and were gone by morning. If I located a nest, I noted it, then called Karen. Once she arrived, I helped stake off the area, stretching pink fluorescent tape along the perimeter. Like a crime scene.

Several years back, Sheldon showed up at one of our meetings with his own maps, with his smug air, and said, "I'm buying this property, gonna build super-size-me condos, and there ain't shit you turtle fuckers can do about it." Okay, that's not exactly what he said, but he may as well have. You get the idea.

Three days passed. No suspects. In the paper, an anonymous source said ample evidence had been collected. Sent to a lab. Had anything else been trapped under Adrienne Blackwater's fingernail besides my skin and blood? Would it even matter? Sheldon was her husband for Christ's sake, so his DNA could easily be explained away. But mine? If I told the absolute, by God, hand-on-a-Bible truth, my story still sounded like a load of crap. I had to do something fast.

I leaned on the glass counter, staring at the assortment of pistols. Also at the guitars, amps, saltwater rods and lures, beach cruisers, and at least one extra-tall unicycle. And jewelry. Lots of jewelry.

"I need ten grand," I said. "You know it's worth double."

Tommy was tall, thin, and had pocked cheeks like a clam shell riddled with worm holes. Lennon glasses hung on the end of his bulbous nose. From a sleeveless flannel, long arms protruded—skinny, smooth, and surprisingly tattoo-less, as if stolen from a pubescent girl. "Ten thousand, huh?" he said, balancing the ring on his fingertips, rotating it as he studied the stones.

"That's a twenty-K ring, Tommy."

"And you're an expert now? An appraiser?"

"Well, no."

"Remind me again why you left Christie's? Why you ditched the auction house to come beachcomb for pennies?"

"Damn, man, what's up your ass today? I'm just looking for a fair shake."

Tommy glared at me and went toward his office, a tightly wrapped ponytail hanging down like a silver rope. When he returned, he placed a photograph on the counter, then tapped the picture with a firm middle finger. "That look familiar to you?"

My stomach clenched. "Jesus, Tommy."

"I said, does that look familiar to you?"

"I swear to God it's been crazy, man. You wouldn't believe what's happened."

"I bet you're right about that."

The picture was a close-up of Adrienne Blackwater's ring, presumably encircling the very finger I'd snatched it from. "Where'd you get that?"

"I should be asking *you* that question," he said, reaching for the ring.

I plucked it off the counter, thought about sprinting out the door. "How long we known each other? Twenty years, right?"

"You think the pigs give a rat's ass how long I've known you, Frank? Detectives dropped this off yesterday," he said, double-tapping the photo for emphasis. "Told me to call immediately if the piece showed up. Well, it showed up all right."

"Christ, Tommy, I had nothing to do with that woman. I know it looks bad but—"

"It looks a whole lot worse than bad, Frank. A shit-ton worse."

"I know."

"You just brought me poison, man. Straight-up hot, boiling poison. And you got the balls to demand ten grand? What the hell's wrong with you, dude? If they hadn't dropped off that pic, I could claim ignorance. But now I'm caught right in the thick of your clusterfuck."

I shook my head, set the ring on the counter. "Listen," I said and then told him the truth. The entire story, all the way back to my Jersey days when my cousin Mickey snapped during that botched job. How two innocent drunks, unbeknown to us, were passed-out in the backseat of the car we'd just boosted. Plain dumb luck. The poor bastards, all groggy and confused, had popped up, startling Mickey. He drew a heater from his waistband and next thing I knew, blood and organs and guts were ruining the upholstery. It was a dark, dark day. Cops picked us up a week later, but by then we'd already planted the gun. The bodies. Set up our boss. Mick had been a smart son of a bitch, I'll give him that.

When I'd finished, Tommy said, "Man, that's heavy." He rubbed his three-day whiskers, thinking hard. "A thousand, Frank. That's the best I can do, then you better get out of Dodge. I'm only offering 'cause Sheldon Blackwater's a cocksucker, and I got no doubt he's responsible. But still, this puts me in a bind, brother. You get me?"

"I get you. And I appreciate it. But can you do me

two for it? I'm flat busted, Tommy. I'm gonna need bank to live on for a while."

"Fifteen-hunge, final offer. It's a dog-eat-dog world out there, my man."

"Yeah, dog-eat-dog all right." Then it hit me. *Dog-eat-dog.* "Deal," I said, and extended my hand to seal the agreement. Tommy was a solid dude.

Raleigh-Durham International was crowded. I was scared to death: of flying, of security, of cops tackling me, grinding my face hard into the floor. But Tommy had coached me on the basics. Belt and shoes removed. Wallet in plastic tray. Backpack on aluminum rollers waiting for scan. I exhaled and nervously walked through the metal detector.

No issues.

I waited, watching the person who controlled the scanner. A black woman, bangs dyed crimson, sitting in a tall chair, staring at her monitor. My backpack was still in there. She motioned for a TSA guard, a super-tall white dude. Broad. Intimidating. He leaned over as she whispered. He nodded, stayed hunched, scoped the monitor as she pointed at the screen. Like referees viewing a replay.

The giant man squinted, pushed his face closer to the monitor, looked up and caught my eyes. Perhaps I was too old for this now, not built for the stress anymore. My poor heart could barely pump the sludgy fat and grime I fed my body every day, let alone deal with this. I swore, right then, that if I escaped, I'd get in shape. Start eating better. Maybe (probably not) quit smoking. The guard reached into the mouth of the machine and retrieved the backpack, holding it away from his body as if carrying a leaking bag of garbage.

"This yours?" he said. No smile, no pleasantness.

"Yeah. Something wrong?"

"Come with me," he said, striding toward a corner table. My mind flickered with multiple doomsday prison scenarios.

"Need your ticket and ID."

I handed him my ticket.

"ID?"

I dug into my pocket. "Shit, my wallet's still over there. In the plastic tray thingy."

"Go get it."

I retrieved it, along with my belt and shoes. Handed him my North Carolina license. It didn't say Frank Trout. I was Mike Agee now, something Tommy had worked up.

The TSA guy looked at my license, then my ticket, and muttered *Hmmmf* or some equivalent.

"What? What is it?"

He put on latex gloves, the cuffs snapping at his colossal wrists. "Open your backpack."

My hands fumbled with the zipper.

He rummaged around, removing a sandwich baggie with my toothbrush, deodorant, snack-sized Fritos, and finally a terrycloth washrag. He unfolded it and pinched the contents between his thumb and pointer. "What exactly is this?"

"That's a...well, it's my good luck charm."

He surveyed the brown eyeball, the pupil staring right back at him. "Jesus," he mumbled, "it takes all kinds." Then, addressing me, "Is it real?"

"Real? Well, yeah, I mean, it's a real glass eye if that's what you're asking."

"It raised a red flag," he said, nodding at the black woman. "Can't hardly blame her for that. We see some weird shit come through." He placed the eyeball back in the washrag. "You might want to wrap this yourself," he said. "Wouldn't want to break it."

"Yeah, sure." I folded the soft cloth around the eye, methodically, as if it were a rare jewel.

"You ever been?" said the TSA man, now friendly as he returned my ticket and license.

"Pardon?"

"Hawaii. Went there for my honeymoon. Paradise, man."

"Oh, yeah, that's what I hear. No, this'll be my first time."

"Well, enjoy your trip, Mr. Agee. Sorry for the inconvenience."

"Not a problem at all," I said. "Mind pointing me toward Gate D?"

One late spring, four years ago, I witnessed a turtle laying her eggs. I'd been combing at night, couldn't sleep, when I discovered the outline of a large mound, barely moving. She was like an enormous ladybug in silhouette. I hunched in the sand, forty feet away. For something so massive, she was amazingly quiet—only a soft *whisk* as her flippers dug the hole before she settled herself in. And then she sat there. We sat there. Both of us staring at the lapping tide, the sea as calm as a lake. We stayed for hours.

As dawn approached, the turtle and I locked eyes— her wise and bulbous ones to my tiny, inferior ones. She'd known I was there all along, and I like to think she'd trusted me. Sensed I was on her side. Maybe understood I'd take care of her eggs. Would protect her babies.

Then she moved. She swept sand over the nest before dragging herself toward the ocean. She entered the water gracefully. A beautiful woman sliding into a bath. And then I cried. Not out of sadness necessarily, just out of awe. At how striking that mama turtle was as her carapace dissolved into the sea, her duty done. How she'd never see her babies again.

I thought about my own mom, who I hadn't contacted since I'd escaped from Jersey. She was still going strong; I'd stalked her on Facebook. There was no way to fathom how much it crushed her, us not talking, not knowing if I was alive. But my silence protected her. I'd always hoped she understood that.

I patrolled the area throughout the summer. In early August the nest dropped, meaning the sand had sunk. That faint depression indicated the hatch was imminent.

Curious vacationers huddled around each evening, questioning me as I kept guard. And that was fine. The more who witnessed the miracle, the more who'd be swayed to oppose the likes of Sheldon Blackwater.

The hatching almost always occurred shortly after sunset, at near dark. I'd clear a path, lining up interested observers on either side, forming a gauntlet toward the ocean. Thrilled children knelt in the sand as the babies left the nest, but it was the adults who were more affected. We volunteers had special red lights, and we explained that absolutely no pictures were allowed because the flash would blind the hatchlings. The turtles had to see the white surf rolling in, which drew them, the same as it had for millennia.

Once the birthing began, I'd shine my red light on the initial little fella who worked his way toward the water. Following the leader, more turtles emerged, all hatching within minutes of each other, then marching by the dozens toward the sea. Each one smaller than my palm, they clumsily trudged, little flippers flapping as they waddled like a hundred miniature Charlie Chaplins, ready and excited for the world. Knowing nothing of its dangers.

I always got worked up during a hatch, but this instance was more profound because I'd been there from the beginning. I proudly watched my babies venture down the beach—my beach—before heading off. That tiny section of sand was the one little spot on this earth where I had contributed something positive to the world.

Where I'd made a difference. Perhaps one or two would survive.

The papers hinted that Sheldon's story wasn't holding up. The cops hadn't been able to locate a single downed telephone pole on the entire island. Sheldon had given a location where he and Adrienne supposedly crashed, then an alternate when the cops pressed, then said he wasn't positive a snapped telephone pole had fallen on his vehicle after all. Perhaps a tree instead. It had been dark, rainy, windy.

No arrests yet, but they were on to him. I was sick, knowing my DNA would provide his high-priced lawyers all the reasonable doubt they'd ever need. Combine those few drops of blood with a smidgen of skin cells, couple that with my hasty disappearance, and the result was obvious. The search for me would ramp up bigtime. How long until a sharp eye picked me out on the airport security cameras, maybe jawing with that TSA agent?

I stuck my forehead to the airplane window as smoke-stacked clouds floated below. I had read on the internet about the endangered green turtles in Hawaii. Maybe Trisha and I would visit one of the black sand beaches, have a picnic with cheese and pineapple and a bottle of wine, then go for a swim with the turtles. Strap on goggles and fins, swim alongside as their wrinkled arms flapped effortlessly, flying in slow motion. Who knows, Trish and I, we might even hold hands.

Maybe we'd patch ourselves up and make another go of it. Well, probably not. But I realized I wanted to find someone I could trust, could be myself with, even if it was only short-lived.

I turned off my movie screen and stuffed the tiny pillow beneath my neck. Since I'd been sixteen, the longest I'd ever gone without a smoke was probably three hours. And that had been hell. I wasn't sure how I'd handle a long flight, wasn't sure how I'd handle anything, really. I took one last look out the window, wedges of vast ocean now visible through the cloud breaks. I was six miles above Earth, screaming through the sky at five hundred miles per hour. Countless glints of sunlight, as if the water's surface was hammered metal, caught my eye in some magical, orchestrated dance. I burned the image into my memory—for the darker days to come—then closed my eyes and re-watched as it took form again.

Pleasant Grove

The snow had just begun to fall when Johnny's mother reminded him for the third time that she had to have milk and eggs. He'd been through fourteen winters in his lifetime, all of them in that same Virginia farmhouse near McPeak Mountain, so he felt he had a pretty good feel for how bad this storm might be. The way the sky hung heavy, the way everything turned gray, the way smoke chugged from the chimney, not in a straight column but instead spilling and hovering over the roof like a witch's brew. By Johnny's calculations, this was going to be a whopper.

"Johnny, we have to have milk," said his mother. "Henry's probably going to close early. If the babies don't have their food, there'll be hell to pay. The milk truck won't deliver in this snow. Not for a few days most likely."

"I know," said Johnny, buttoning his mackintosh and securing a wool toboggan on his head. "I'm going."

His mother reached into her coin purse and handed him four quarters. "Get as much as you can carry, and a dozen eggs. The hens aren't laying good in this cold."

"All right, Ma," said Johnny as he threw a canvas

rucksack over his shoulder and headed out the door.

Those babies. Those damn babies. They were enough to drive him insane. What his mother meant, what his mother called her babies, were the eight or nine or maybe ten cats, Johnny wasn't even sure anymore, that ruled his mother's life. They ate better than he did most days, and he resented them for it. There'd been many a time, while his mother was at work, where he'd considered taking the twenty gauge and culling the kitty population by a few. But he'd never mustered the courage. Not yet, anyway. But the anger and bitterness was building.

He cursed those cats as he headed toward Henry's General Store—the dirt and gravel already covered in a thin layer of snow—working his way through the Pleasant Grove section of McPeak Mountain. It was the only store on the mountain, and he knew his mother was right: Henry often closed shop early, for any reason he wanted, though usually it was because he'd run out of liquor and needed to get home to refill. So an impending snowstorm was a perfect excuse.

The temperature wasn't cold, barely freezing, and no wind to speak of. The flakes fell straight down, fat and heavy, as Johnny trudged along, his boots giving that comforting crunching sound as they marched through the absolute quiet. Johnny loved the silence that a snowstorm brought. No birds chirping, no cars straining up the hill, no clopping of horse hooves or creaking wagon wheels from old-timey farmers who still stubbornly resisted the purchase of a tractor.

The road was narrow and hilly, twisting through stands of oak and pine. Henry's was only a mile away, but in the snow everything took longer, and besides, Johnny was in no hurry. During the walk home, it would be a different story, wanting to remove the weight of the glass bottles, but at the moment he was in no rush. At the moment, he was going to enjoy it.

He stopped at the little stone bridge crossing Oldfield Creek and stared downstream, seeing rounded white mounds on the exposed stones. He often came down here to set legholds for mink, raccoons, and muskrat, selling the pelts to Henry for spending money. But he preferred using snares, which he set in the fields near his house, occasionally catching the ultimate prize: a red fox.

As the creek gurgled, as the snow continued to fall, now catching on the overhanging sycamore limbs curling over the water, he wondered if his daddy had ever trapped. He wondered if his love for the hunt was inherited. He thought about that often when he was in the woods, imagining what his dad had been like, fantasizing about how different his life would be if his father hadn't been killed during a training exercise in the Army. His mother had told him she was still pregnant when his father died, at a barracks in South Carolina, never even getting the opportunity to go overseas to kill some Nazis. She only had one photo, a handsome man in uniform, his face turned in profile. But Johnny felt he resembled his father and hoped to one day have the same strong jaw line, those same rugged features.

The high whine of an approaching pickup snapped him from his reverie. The engine raced and the truck moved fast, sliding down the hill toward the bridge, the back end fishtailing. It was an older model, probably a '50 or '51, and definitely a Ford, judging by the rounded roof and distinct eyeball headlights.

Johnny had to make a decision and make it fast. The truck now careened from side-to-side, out of control, the man frantically working his hands over the steering wheel, trying to right the ship. But it wasn't going to happen; that ship was destined to sink.

Johnny hopped onto the stone wall and leapt, dropping eight feet before landing feet-first in the creek. His outstretched hands plunked into the icy water as his momentum propelled him forward, but he avoided falling flat on his face. At the same instant, a terrific crash sounded above. Steel collided with stone, then a horrible scraping as sparks showered over the bridge, ending with a deadening thud as the truck slammed into a massive oak.

Johnny's boots sucked up the shallow creek before he managed to climb the gentle embankment toward the road. Steam hissed from beneath the crumpled hood, and the snow, which was hammering now, disappeared like magic as it met the hot steel.

Fog clouded the driver's window, preventing Johnny from seeing inside. He looked around, hoping someone would mysteriously appear. To help. To take over. To tell him what to do. But all he saw was a column of peaceful hemlocks lining the road, their boughs holding soft pillows of snow. So he grabbed the handle and pulled, but the door, caved-in and showing fresh streaks of silver in the red paint, was stuck. He tugged harder, throwing his weight into it, and the door opened awkwardly, sending off a horrendous squeak and pop through the silence.

Inside, the man sat slumped over the bent and broken steering wheel, the top nearly touching the dashboard, almost as if it had melted. The windshield had fractured like pond ice, the epicenter containing pieces of hair and skin and blood. Johnny had never seen a dead person before, but he calmly grabbed at the wool collar of the man's red-checked hunting jacket, pulling him back so he could sit properly. It seemed the right thing to do. The driver's head lolled as if devoid of neck muscles, finally resting against the cold rear window, his bloody chin pointing toward the roof.

Johnny hadn't recognized the truck as one he'd seen around town before, nor could he identify the man. But he didn't figure anyone, not even a best friend or wife, could have ID'd him right then. His smashed nose had shifted to the left. A large piece of skin was absent from his forehead, presumably clinging to the windshield, and mashed wire from his glasses had wedged into his cheeks, though somehow the lenses had stayed intact. His entire face, from forehead to chin, was sopping with blood, and a pool of it stained the thighs of his dungarees.

At first Johnny thought for sure the man had to be dead, but then he noticed subtle movement. Breathing.

Then a slow gurgling emerged, similar to Oldfield Creek rolling over the rocks.

"Mister, can you hear me? Mister, you okay?"

No response. Johnny wasn't sure what to do but figured since he was halfway between home and Henry's, the smartest thing would be to continue on. His mother didn't have a telephone, but Henry did, and he could call the police. Except, just as Johnny was about to leave, he looked across the man's lap and noticed something on the passenger's side floorboard. A beige gunnysack. And spilling from the top, where the drawstring had loosened, gobs of twenty dollar bills fanned-out like tail feathers.

Johnny ran around to the other side, where the passenger door opened easily. Without forethought of repercussions, he snatched the bag and stuffed it inside his rucksack. And that's when he saw the pistol on the floor, lying there like a curious, shiny object. Before thinking properly, he grabbed that, too. As he went to close the door, the man said, "I see you, boy." The voice was strained, weak. But Johnny heard it all the same.

He slammed the door, ran to the bridge, and tossed the pistol as far as he could downstream. Then he took off for home, shuffling through the snow—now boot-high and rising fast—practicing the words he'd tell his mother once he arrived. "Henry's was already closed, Ma. I'm sorry. I know I messed up."

* * *

That evening, once he was sure his mother had gone to sleep, he pulled the bag from the back corner of his closet, where he'd hidden it beneath empty shoe boxes and a mound of dusty quilts. He dumped the cash onto his bed and stacked the crisp twenties into piles of ten. When he'd finished, he couldn't believe the tally. He counted it again, and then again, before he uttered aloud, "Four thousand eight hundred dollars."

Johnny didn't sleep well, tossing and turning, wondering about the man. Wondering if he was still alive. Most importantly, wondering if he—Johnny—would get caught.

The next morning, when there was a pounding on the front door, his heart screamed. He scrambled out of bed, slapped on clothes, and tried to beat his mother to the door, not at all sure what he'd do once he got there. Especially if it was the man.

But it wasn't the man. Instead, standing on the front porch was the local sheriff, dressed in a heavy coat and wide-brimmed hat. "Hey, son," said the sheriff. "Your mama at home?"

"Yes, sir," he said, his heart screaming louder still, his cheeks flushing as he turned to yell for her. But she was already there, directly behind him, wiping her wet hands on the bottom of an apron, her hair pulled up tightly in a bun. One of the cats walked figure-eights through her legs, arching its back as it brushed the hem of her dress.

"Hey, Bryson," said his mother. "What brings you here in such pretty weather?"

"Patricia," said the sheriff, pinching the hat's edge

and nodding. "Was wondering if I might talk to you for a minute."

"Come on in. Get out of the cold. You want coffee?"

"No, I'm okay." He stamped his boots on the porch boards, knocking out clods of frozen snow.

Johnny looked out at the front yard before closing the door behind the sheriff. The morning was overcast, but the snow had stopped. He figured a foot and a half or more; his tracks should have easily been covered. At least he hoped so.

The sheriff followed Patricia into the kitchen where she pulled out a chair for him at the table. He took it while she grabbed the hot kettle from the stove. Johnny sat down at the far end, staring at the hulking figure of the sheriff. All he could think about was the load of money in his room, second guessing whether he'd put it back in the closet or left it sitting out.

She poured two cups of coffee, despite the sheriff's refusal, and set one in front of him. He warmed his hands around the mug before taking a sip.

"Johnny, you need to go get your chores started," said Patricia as she sat down. "Sheriff needs to talk to me."

Before Johnny could rise, the sheriff said, "Actually, he ought to stay. He needs to hear this too."

Johnny's cheeks flushed, his breathing went short, figuring the sheriff must know everything. Figured he'd found the man, the man told him that some boy had stolen his money, and the sheriff followed the tracks right to the front door.

"Last night one of my deputies located a truck by the Oldfield Creek bridge. Crashed into a tree. Torn up pretty good. Looks like the fella lost control coming down the hill. Not sure how long it'd been there, but the tire tracks were already covered by the time my man arrived."

Johnny discretely exhaled.

"The driver okay?" asked Patricia with a look of mild interest, but not overly so. Instead, her expression seemed to say, *So why are you telling me this?*

"I don't know if he's okay or not. He wasn't in the truck. There were some faint boot prints in the snow, but they'd pretty much filled up by the time I arrived. And a fair amount of blood. Looks like he went to the creek and washed up before he took off. But here's the thing. The truck was stolen. Was the getaway vehicle in a robbery yesterday. The guy knocked-off the bank over in Floyd. Got away with nearly five grand."

Patricia took a sip of her coffee, her eyes showing a little more interest. "And you think he might've come here?"

"I don't think so. I scouted around your place before I knocked. Didn't see any sign. But he's around here somewhere. We're trying to get some dogs from over in Christiansburg, but with the snow, everything's at a standstill. I just wanted to make you aware. He's got a pistol. Used it during the heist. You got a gun, don't you? And a vehicle?"

Patricia glanced over at Johnny, suddenly showing more concern. "The alternator's gone bad on the car.

Haven't had the money to fix it. We've got a shotgun."

"What about a phone?"

"No, no phone," she said. "You got any idea who you're looking for? A description or something there abouts?"

The sheriff hesitated, sipped his coffee, then scratched his nails across the table grooves. "Well, here's the other thing," he said, talking to the table instead of her. "We've got a pretty good notion that the fella, the fella we're looking for, is Martin."

For the first time, Johnny saw a look of true fear slide across his mother's face. Her eyes widened, her jaw went slack. Johnny reacted similarly. Because he recognized the name, though it made no sense.

"What...what do you mean?" she said.

"That's the real reason I'm here," said the sheriff, finally making eye contact. "Considering the truck is only a mile away, we think he was probably coming here, looking for a hideout. You probably didn't know, but he's been locked up at Petersburg the past five years. For another robbery."

Patricia barely nodded. She said, almost a whisper now, "I heard something about it."

"Well, two days ago he escaped. Warden called and alerted us."

"Bryson, I haven't seen that man in fifteen years." Her voice was suddenly sharp. Angry. "Why would he come here? If he does, I'll blast him to Kingdom Come. I swear to God I will."

"I'm not accusing you."

34

"You can search the entire house if you don't believe me. I wouldn't put him up for nothing."

"Patricia," said the sheriff, showing both hands as if slowing traffic, "I'm only here to warn you. You two need to be on your guard. We'll run patrols, get a search party going. But with this snow, it's going to take time. From the looks of the accident and all the blood, he couldn't't've made it too far. He's probably banged up pretty good. Could've frozen last night for all I know."

"That man's tougher than a pine knot. You know that, Bryson. He eats barbed-wire pie for breakfast, smiles while chewing it. If he's got a pile of money to warm his bones, he's not about to crawl up and die."

"Soon as we catch him, you'll be the first to know. In the meantime, keep that shotgun handy."

Patricia walked the sheriff to the door while Johnny remained at the table. He had so many questions. So many thoughts. *What's going on? Who's Martin? That was my daddy's name.*

Patricia sat back down at the kitchen table after showing the sheriff out. She raised her coffee cup but couldn't steady her hands to take a sip. "Johnny, baby, we need to have a little talk. There's something I have to tell you."

His father, as it turned out, hadn't been killed in the Army. Instead, he'd been a cheating, lying scoundrel who'd left Patricia once he learned he'd swollen her belly. Disappeared, leaving her with nothing.

"And the picture of the soldier?" Johnny had asked. "Who was that?"

Patricia's tears showed her anguish. But also her relief, it seemed to Johnny. Her secret a secret no more. "That was my brother. Your Uncle Bruno. He was the one killed in South Carolina."

Johnny was confused, betrayed, and couldn't figure out what to do. He wandered to his room, checked on the money, then attempted to wrap his mind around all he'd learned. If his mother wanted to keep secrets from him, then he had a nearly five thousand dollar secret he'd keep from her. But after some stewing, he became restless and unsatisfied, thinking of new questions, so he went back and grilled his mother for more answers. By late afternoon, they were both exhausted. Emotionally drained.

"Those chickens need feeding," his mother said as dusk settled in. "In fact, why don't you kill one and I'll make us a hot soup. They aren't laying for squat anyway. We could use a hearty meal."

"Okay," said Johnny, thinking that getting outside might do him some good.

"Bring the gun."

"I'm only going to the coop. It'll take five minutes."

"Bring the gun," she repeated, and he knew enough not to argue.

With the shotgun slung over his shoulder, Johnny sloughed through the high snow until he entered the chicken coop. He let his eyes adjust, then scanned the shack before standing the gun in the corner. He removed the feed barrel lid and tossed a few handfuls into the fenced-in area. The kibble sprinkled the snow, and Johnny laughed for the first time that day as the chickens scrambled out the door, trying not to sink, flapping their wings furiously as if avoiding drowning.

For twenty minutes, he kept himself occupied by tossing out handfuls of grain, having a little fun with the chickens. He was in the process of sweeping the coop, his mind still abuzz, when a commotion sounded from the house. Pots and pans clattered, and at first he thought his mother had had an accident, probably dropping the soup pot. But then she yelled. Yelled for him. Followed by a man's voice, angry and agitated.

Johnny grabbed the twenty gauge and ran for the kitchen. When he entered, the man he'd seen the day before, his own father, stood near the stove, a knife in hand. His mother was backed into the corner by the cupboard, shivering as if cold, gripping a cast iron skillet.

The man turned to face Johnny, looking better than the day before but still a complete mess. He'd fixed his glasses the best he could, but they were still bent and hung askew from the bridge of his mashed nose. The wide gash on his forehead was pink and raw but no longer bleeding, his clothes stained with crusty blood.

"Listen, boy, I just want my money. Tell me where it's at and I'll leave y'all alone." His voice was stronger than yesterday. His face hard, his eyes harder. He glanced at the shotgun pointing at his chest but didn't seem concerned. He'd strategically positioned himself in front of

Patricia, so that if Johnny pulled the trigger, she'd be sprayed with birdshot too.

"He doesn't have your God-blessed money, Martin," she yelled, her neck tendons strained taut like piano wire, the skillet wielded in front of her like a sword.

"Yes, he does," he said calmly. It was like he knew he was going to get his money back, now it was only a matter of how much blood needed to be spilled first. He shifted his eyes back-and-forth between Johnny and Patricia, squeezing the knife. "He stole it from my truck. Didn't even bother to help me, Patty. Just took the money and ran. But I recognized him right off. Had blood running down my face, dripping in my eyes, but even still, saw right off he was the spitting image of his mama."

Martin took a slow step away from Patricia and shuffled, with a subtle limp, toward Johnny. Johnny, in turn, stepped back, performing an awkward dance ritual, keeping the gun trained at Martin's chest.

"You saw the wrong boy," said Patricia, almost pleading. "Johnny was here with me all day yesterday. He doesn't have your money."

"Tell her, boy. *Johnny*, is it? Tell her how you took my sack of money," he said, smiling a little. "Tell her, *son*."

"It wasn't me," said Johnny, wondering if Martin noticed the barrel quivering. "I didn't take your money."

"Oh, but you did. You took it, and I want it back. Show me where it's at, and I'll give you some. A little reward. Then I'll be gone."

"I didn't take it."

Martin moved forward another step, now only a few feet from the tip of the barrel. "You wouldn't shoot your old man, now would you? Your dear old daddy?"

Quicker than Johnny thought possible, especially for a man in Martin's condition, he snatched for the shotgun like a striking snake. And then Johnny felt his own shoulder blades slam into the wall. The pleasant smell of cordite clouded the kitchen, and Johnny's ears rang from the explosion in such close quarters.

Martin lay curled on the slats of the pine floor, blood seeping into the cracks, meandering like raindrops on a windshield. A couple of cats scurried away, taking cover. Patricia shot from her corner, the frying pan gripped in both hands above her head, and brought it down on Martin's left ear with a dull, solid thud. For good measure.

Johnny leaned against the wall, the gun still pointed at Martin, his shoulder aching from the kickback.

"You just killed your daddy, Johnny." She didn't say it in accusatory fashion. She didn't say it happily either. Just matter-of-fact.

"I'm sorry, Ma. I thought he was going to hurt you. Us."

"That son-of-a-bitch has been dead to me for years, baby." She kneeled over the body, surveying, but still held the skillet at the ready. When she was satisfied, she looked up. "Now where'd you hide that money?"

Johnny hesitated, realizing the gun was pointed at his mother now.

"You're not in trouble," she said, her voice soothing. Calming. The same way she often purred to the cats. "Just tell me."

He hesitated again. "It's in my room. In my closet."

"Good," said Patricia, nodding with an almost imperceptible smile. "Now let's find a better hiding spot. Then we'll figure out what to do with him."

Len had been a young teenager when the huge snowstorm hit McPeak Mountain shortly before Christmas. One morning, a day or two after the storm, his father advised that Len needed to cut down a Christmas tree for the family. Being the oldest of the three children, and the only boy, he was thrilled to do so. It was his first time setting out on his own with such an important job, and it made him feel like his father recognized he was becoming a man. He relished the responsibility and didn't want to disappoint.

He bundled up, received an apple-butter sandwich from his mother, and along with a canteen and an oiled crosscut saw from the horse barn, set off through the deep snow. The sun was out, the sky a deep blue, emphasizing that the front had indeed passed.

Len knew exactly where he was going. He often spent time in the woods, sometimes hunting, more often just hiking to see what he could see. If he crossed the pasture behind the farm, and then climbed the formidable wooded hill, there was a nice stand of white pine running along the ridgeline; the ridge that marked the edge of his property line; the ridge separating his land from several other families sparsely located in that little section of Pleasant Grove. Directly on the other side of the ridge, nestled at the foot of McPeak Mountain, was a small farmhouse where a mother and her son lived, the father having run off years ago.

By the time Len made it to the top of the ridge, he'd already unbuttoned his jacket and let it flap open at his hips. He'd removed his watchman's cap and stuffed it into his back pocket as sweat trickled along his neck. He took a drink of water and then decided that he'd explore a little before he cut the tree down. It was going to be an all-day affair, what with the depth of the snow and having to drag the tree nearly a mile home, so he had no reason to rush. Besides, the longer he was gone, the more chores his sisters would have to cover for him. Len was no fool.

There was an old, abandoned woodcutter's cabin that he frequented from time to time when he was out in the woods. A place he and his sisters would sometimes play. A place that Len thought of as his own. The foundation was made of granite, the fireplace comprised of similar stone, while the structure itself had been built with roughly hewn poplar. When his sisters weren't around, Len still enjoyed going there by himself, mainly because he'd stashed a pile of girly magazines beneath some rotted floorboards. And they weren't just standard run-of-the-mill magazines, where women might be scantily clad but certainly didn't show any nipples. No, these were underground magazines. From France or some other exotic place. Showing women in all their glory. And not only women, but men, too. Men who were doing unspeakable things to these women. Things that Len and his school buddies often talked about when far from the ears of adults, but certainly not things he'd ever seen or been a part of.

So that's where he was headed. It was an easy walk of about a half mile along the ridgeline. At least it was easy when there wasn't high snow to slog through. But a boy's urges are strong at that age, and an extra half mile of trudging through snow was a small price to pay.

He'd made it about half-way, keeping his eyes down and following a set of deer tracks when a noise at the bottom of the slope startled him. Len had spent enough time in the woods to know the difference between the natural sounds of the forest and those manmade. And this one was definitely human. He couldn't discern it exactly, but whatever it was, there was a distinct ring of metal glancing off something hard.

With every step he took, it got louder; a rhythmic clatter keeping nearly perfect cadence. Len slowed and walked as quietly as he could. Before long, with his eyes trained down the mountainside, he finally located the noise. At the base of the hill, smack in the middle of the forest, were two figures. One was a hunched woman, wrapped in a shawl, and the other was a thin young man, about the same size as Len, standing by her side as she worked at a bare patch of ground, dropping mounds of dirt onto the otherwise white blanket of the woods. The sound was slightly delayed as it carried up the hillside, but Len saw that the woman was diligently digging a hole. After a few more shovelfuls, she passed the tool to the boy and he took over.

Len knelt in the snow, hiding behind a pine. He was thrilled and exhilarated. Thoughts of the cabin and magazines no longer mattered because once he settled in, he realized there was a third figure among the other two. But this third figure lay slightly off to the side, facedown in the snow.

Len knew exactly who the people were. Well, he knew who the two people still *alive* were. It would take another week of reading newspapers and asking innocent questions of his parents about what had ever happened to Johnny's father, over on the other side of the hill, before Len put it all together.

But at that moment, he was mesmerized. A dead body. And two people, a mother and son, attempting to bury that body. Judging by the snow trough that ended at the man's feet, the trough that wound through the trees and back toward Johnny's farmhouse, the man certainly hadn't walked into those woods on his own. It wasn't like Johnny and his mother had found the man lying there while out looking for their own Christmas tree. No, he'd been dragged, and whatever they were up to, it clearly wasn't noble or altruistic.

The pair struggled mightily to pull the dead man toward the hole, each grabbing an arm before finally rolling him into the excavated rectangle. They collapsed next to the grave once they'd dropped him in, not out of any grief it seemed, but simply out of pure exhaustion.

There was no telling how long they'd been working, but considering they'd dragged him through the snow a good half mile from the farmhouse—assuming that's where he'd died—then dug a deep hole in frozen ground, it was no surprise they were worn out.

They each fisted snow and stuffed it into their mouths like handfuls of popcorn at the picture house. Len couldn't discern their words, but he imagined the conversation. Before too long, they returned to work, laboring to refill the hole. When they were nearly finished, Johnny grabbed something the size of a large cigar box. He opened the lid, took a peek inside, then carefully placed the box in the grave. He and his mother filled the hole, then covered it with soggy leaves before finally tossing snow over top and smoothing it out. Like frosting a cake.

If Len hadn't witnessed it with his own eyes, he'd have never noticed the area looking strange or out of the ordinary, except maybe the trough snaking through the trees. But some wind and another snowfall would erase that in no time. All things considered, they'd covered their tracks pretty well.

He waited until they'd both walked away before he left his perch behind the pine trunk and headed down the hill. He'd learned early on that being privy to other people's secrets could work to his advantage. He'd used the method repeatedly when he had dirt on his sisters; dirt they didn't want their parents to know. So he couldn't predict how he might use Johnny's secret, but he knew he'd keep his mouth shut for now. Something as big as this might prove quite profitable someday. Not to mention, as soon as he felt sure Johnny and his mother weren't coming back, he planned to find out what was in that buried box.

That winter had been an especially brutal one for Johnny and his mother. It seemed that every time the snow had nearly melted, a new storm dumped another foot. Which wasn't necessarily a bad thing. Every fresh snowfall helped keep the secret hidden.

Before they'd buried Martin, along with the money, Johnny's mother had decided to keep four hundred dollars for expenses—unpaid bills, groceries, to get the car fixed. They had no idea if the money had been marked by the bank, but by using a twenty here or there down at Henry's General Store, they figured they weren't in much danger of getting caught. The sheriff had occasionally stopped by—the first time only three days after Johnny had shot his father—to inform them that they hadn't located Martin. He said he imagined Martin had either frozen to death or bled to death, and his body would probably be found after the spring melt.

By mid-March, the snow had indeed disappeared, but his mother advised they leave the money where it was for the time being. They were in no need at the moment, and the longer they let things settle, the safer they'd be. But that all changed after the engine on the recently repaired car seized in late April. It had to be towed down the mountain to a mechanic in Floyd who informed

Patricia that the transmission was ruined and beyond repair. Since she had to have a car to get to work, the solution was obvious.

"You need to dig the box up," she informed him after school one day. "I think we're safe now. Besides, I'd rather have it hidden in the house than in the middle of the woods. Or maybe under the chicken coop. Doesn't matter. We'll figure that out. What's important is that we have it nearby."

He grabbed a shovel from the shed, slung it over his shoulder like a hobo with a bindle, and set out through the woods. It was a perfect spring day, warm with blue skies and a bit of a breeze rustling the tops of the trees. The poplar leaves were as big as squirrels' ears, and the oaks had already formed their pollen filled strings, reminding Johnny of pipe cleaners, which drifted to the ground when the wind gusted. Johnny enjoyed the walk, loving the woods as they came back to life after the winter. He even loved the mud and muck of a bog he had to tramp through to get to his father's burial site. The beginnings of skunk cabbage had sprouted, their little green heads poking through the mud, and Johnny stamped on everyone he saw, sending off a strong, pungent odor.

When he made it to a dumping ground where old-timers had tossed their steel beer cans, brown medicine bottles, and rusted appliances, Johnny took a left and headed toward the foot of the hill. He'd always been fascinated with the dumping ground, wondering who had put all that garbage there. There were no houses around, other than an abandoned cabin on the ridge, so he'd never been able to figure out why anyone would have chosen that place to dump their trash. Regardless, as a younger boy, he'd enjoyed rummaging around the dump site, imagining in his boyhood fantasies that he might discover some sort of hidden treasure.

But today, as he left the dump behind, he was in search of an actual hidden treasure. He was excited to uncover the iron lock box, open it, and run his fingers all over that beautiful cash. The cash that would buy him some decent clothes so he wouldn't get made fun of at school. The cash that would enable him to purchase candy bars and maybe even the occasional T-bone steak. The cash that would send him to Virginia Polytechnic Institute and get him out of the poor, depressed confines of Pleasant Grove. Confines that offered no sort of future. In short, the cash that would ensure that he and his mother would escape poverty, once and for all.

So he was excited to dig up the money, get back home, and count it. Over and over. Just sit there and stack each and every bill into little piles, the same as he'd done that day on his bed. The events of those few days, of the truck crashing, of him taking the money, of finding out the man's identity, of then blowing the guts out of that same man, his father, of dragging him through the snow and burying him, all of those events had haunted him. But it had gotten better with every passing week. The memories weren't quite as sharp, the guilt subsided, and there was always that pot of gold at the end of the rainbow. That's what really made it easier to deal with. That, and knowing that his father would have most likely killed him and his mother if he hadn't pulled the trigger. That's certainly the way his mother had rationalized it to him on those cold nights when they'd huddled around the woodstove and the subject had come up. They'd talked about it often for the first few weeks, until finally his mother had laid down an ultimatum, saying it was time to move forward. What was done was done and they had to try to forget about it. To be thankful that Johnny's sorry excuse for a father had at least been able to provide them with something before he died, especially considering that for the past fourteen years he'd never given them as much as a penny.

But as he neared the spot where he'd buried both his father and the money, his excitement turned to one of dread. The idea of being alone in the woods with the body of his dead father didn't seem so appealing. Yes, the day was beautiful, but deep in the woods it was almost impossible to see the sky. And every time the wind blew and the tree limbs slapped against one another, eerily clicking and clacking, he shuddered. He realized he couldn't tell if other people might be shuffling around in the woods. Might be hiding, waiting to jump him and steal the money.

And even worse was the realization that he was about to dig up a grave. His father's grave. Yes, the iron box was right on top and he shouldn't come close to the decaying corpse, but what if the ground had shifted? What if the box had sunk during the snowmelt, when the soil had gotten soft and saturated? What if he glimpsed his father's dead face, the flesh rotting and peeling from the skull? What if there really was such a thing as ghosts?

At the foot of a steep hill, Johnny located the area where he and his mother had dug. He'd always been good in the woods, knew how to remember landmarks, and in this instance, the marker was a forked trunk maple. When he'd originally picked the spot, he'd stood with his back to the tree before walking six paces. Then he'd started digging.

But he didn't have to recount his paces this time because, much to his surprise, the dirt still looked relatively fresh. Dead, windblown leaves had covered the area, but if someone who was really an expert in the woods—like the sheriff, for example—had seen the partially exposed patch, they would have easily recognized that it wasn't natural. That something was off. Which bothered him. If the sheriff decided to get a search party together sometime soon, the grave might be detected.

These new thoughts, of getting caught, suddenly superseded his previous ideas about ghosts and rotting flesh, so he immediately stuck his shovel into the earth, amazed by how soft it was. How easy the digging was. Only five minutes in, he felt and heard the steel of his shovel clink against the lockbox. And what a beautiful sound it was. Like the till of a cash register sliding open, offering up its riches.

Johnny dug around the perimeter of the box, then got on his knees, grabbed the edges, and shifted it back and forth as he loosed it from the rich, dark soil. He brushed away the dirt, then unstuck muddy clumps and clods attached to the hinges. When it was nearly clean, he blew across the top as if extinguishing a candle, removing the last tiny particles.

As he raised the lid, he would've much rather seen ghosts and goblins and wicked spirits rise from the ground than what he saw instead. He would have rather smelled his father's decaying flesh, would have rather had witches creep from behind the trees and boil him in water. Because the box was empty. The cash—all those crisp twenty dollar bills—was gone. A vacuum of empty space. Nothing. Absolutely nothing.

Johnny rapidly closed the box, then opened it again as if prying apart an oyster, hoping that he'd been mistaken and this time he'd find the pearl. But there was no pearl. He tossed the box aside and began digging with his hands. His fingers worked through the soil, spraying the surrounding dead leaves as he pawed like a dog after a bone. Maybe, he thought, the money had somehow fallen out when he'd dropped it in the grave. Maybe the money hadn't been in the box to begin with, though he was positive it had been. He remembered taking one last glance before carefully setting the box in place. He dug deeper and deeper, no longer caring if he ran into his father's remains. He frantically slung dirt out of the hole, ripping earthworms in half, scratching his fingers against small stones until they bled. But it was no use. The money was gone.

He almost vomited as he dejectedly filled-in the hole,

his effort half-hearted. He knew he had to make the scene look perfect. Knew he couldn't afford to be lazy, but he simply didn't care. At that moment, prison seemed like as good a place as any to spend the rest of his days. When he'd finished sprinkling the area with clumps of dead leaves, he grabbed the box and shovel and turned to go, his mind racing. There was only one answer, and rage and anger grew as the idea became more and more of a reality. There was only one possibility. Only one person could have known about the money. Only one person could have taken it.

He gripped the shovel handle tightly as he stormed back toward the house, feeling the weight of the spade as it hung over his shoulder. It would make as good a weapon as any. And if his mother didn't fess up immediately, he might just bring the edge of that heavy blade down and across her neck. Because she'd betrayed him. He knew it for a fact. As the demons swirled in his brain, they convinced him that his mother had double-crossed him. They also convinced him that he'd be a fool if he let her get away with it.

Shooting Creek

Lila

I remember the incident like it was yesterday, back when Winston had been a perfectly normal child. Just another boy growing up in the Virginia mountains. A country boy like any other, running around in the woods, helping Dale with chores, hunting and fishing from the time he could walk pretty much. But that all ended one summer evening shortly after his tenth birthday.

He sat in the other rocking chair on the front porch, snapping beans with me. The sun had fallen behind the trees, but the light hadn't faded away entirely. It was one of those nice evenings, cool and pleasant after a blistering day. Better being out on the porch than inside where the heat was still trapped. That was one thing about living in the Blue Ridge. In July it might get hot as blue blazes, but when night came, that mountain air would brush down the ridges and sweep into the hollow like cool water over river rocks.

The ting of metal on metal, followed by the occasional laugh, sounded from around the corner as Dale and Granddaddy Davis pitched shoes near the chicken coop. The sweet smell of pipe tobacco wafted onto the porch as Winston and I snapped the ends off the beans, both of us rocking in our chairs. He seemed to get right much pleasure in tossing the spent ends over the railing and high into the air. As the dusk settled in, bats swept down and attacked the bean tips in hopes of snatching a mosquito. He'd laugh when he tricked them, and I'd smile now and again as I continued working. We had a pile that needed to be finished before I started canning in the morning, but I wasn't in such a hurry that my boy couldn't get a little enjoyment from the chore.

When dusk had made itself snug and comfortable over the hollow, lightning bugs began flashing their signal around the property. Out in the hay fields; along the tree line on the far side of Shooting Creek; in the void of the tire swing. Winston spoke excitedly when the lightshow began. "Mama, can I go get some?"

Shadows now hid his face from view, so it only seemed logical that he, in turn, couldn't see my smile. But he probably heard it in my voice. "You go on ahead."

Winston jumped off the porch and reached for his Mason jar hidden underneath the bottom stair. He unscrewed the top and gagged from the overpowering stench of yesterday's dead grasshoppers. I even smelled it up on the porch. Like pond muck dredged up from the bottoms. He dumped the old bugs and scrambled off around the side of the house.

Now I don't know exactly what happened next. Of

course Dale and I went over it a thousand times afterwards. Him painfully replaying it like a broken record until I finally told him enough was enough. So I'm speculating on this little stretch between Winston running off and the screams from Dale a few minutes later. High pitched screams that bubbled my skin worse than fork tines on a china plate. "Lila! Oh, Lord God! Lila, get over here quick." But this is what I figure. Winston had managed to trap a few bugs in his jar and was in hot pursuit of another, paying attention to nothing else, when the horseshoe slammed into the soft, delicate spot on the side of his head. He never saw it coming. He dropped to the ground like a heavy sack of flour and *snap*, just like that, my entire world changed.

Sheriff Sutphin

The little community of Shooting Creek is a good fifteen miles from town, way out in the hills. Nothing there but Dehart's Grocery and an old bridge that spans Shooting Creek Gorge. Get some tourists from the Parkway who like to go to the bridge and take pictures. Pretty magnificent sight, really, that bridge hovering a hundred feet above the water.

I was a brand new sheriff then, back around 1980, just a young buck cutting my teeth. I'd seen plenty of crazy stuff when I'd worked for the city of Samford, but going out to the Quesenberry place was one of the sadder things I'd ever been a part of. It's always tough when there's little ones involved.

I'd been patrolling near the Parkway when the call came in over the radio, so I arrived only ten minutes after everything happened. When I reached the end of the Quesenberry's driveway and pulled up to the farmhouse, the evening was just going from can-see to can't-see. I made out a few figures milling about, and when I spotlighted them, they were hovering over a body. Before I even got out of the patrol car, I radioed for an ambulance.

Dale and Lila were both a mess. Shaking, lips quivering, tears streaming down his face but none down hers. She seemed to be in shock, eyes wide and panicked when I shone my flashlight. Her hair tucked away under a kerchief, her hands forming a ball beneath her chin. The graybeard—Lila's granddaddy—was the one hunched over and attending to the boy. Frail man, his overalls hanging off like he'd stolen them from a scarecrow. His old, skinny hands curled as he smoothed the boy's hair back from the wound. Blood streaming and pooling in the boy's ear, his hair matted like wet dog fur. Eyes closed. Skin pale. Ghostly to be sure, but he was still breathing, that I could see. And he was a big boy, too, especially for only ten years old. Nearly as big as his daddy already. You could tell that boy was going to be a horse. Probably would've been able to bale a whole field of hay on his own once he got older if things hadn't turned out the way they did.

When I approached, both Dale and Lila started hollering at me so as I couldn't hardly catch a word. But I got the gist. Horseshoe conked the boy, Winston, right in the head. As I moved the light around in the grass, a U-shaped glint caught the beam and flashed back at me. I think that's what unnerved me more than anything else, seeing that shoe so close to Winston's head.

To the right of him, turned on its side, was a Ball Mason, a couple of pale yellow flashes blinking inside. Seeing those firefly lights, already fading in the jar, gave a gloomy picture of things to come. Like purple storm clouds stacked and rolling up over the mountains.

Ambulance arrived not too long after, and they packed him up and shipped him off. Had to travel over an hour to the hospital in Roanoke, and I expect that might have had something to do with Winston's outcome. That delay.

Six months later I'd be right back on the property again. But that's the nature of the business. Gets a man down every now and again, dealing with other people's sorrow all the time.

Lila

It didn't take me long to figure out that Winston wasn't ever going to be the same. Deep down, it's every mother's hope that their baby won't ever grow up, so in that respect I guess I got my wish. They say be careful what you wish for because you just might get it. I suppose that's true.

He was in the hospital for two weeks, and I lived in that room the entire time. Dale made it over once or twice, but he had to keep the farm up—that's what he said anyway—and I understood. The poor man felt awful, blamed himself for everything, and wasn't dealing with it all that well. On the few occasions he did stop by, he had liquor on his breath, which really got me concerned. I didn't blame him one iota for what had happened, and I'd told him as much, but it didn't seem to do a thing for his conscience.

The good news was, Winston didn't remember anything. And other than some headaches early on, he wasn't in pain. As far as he knew, he'd gone out to catch lightning bugs, then fallen asleep. When he'd woken up, it was like he'd lost a few years, but overall he was happy. And innocent. That was the big thing. Doctor said he would essentially be a ten-year-old the rest of his life. He'd keep growing, would look like an adult, but his mind would never advance.

But he wasn't stupid. I realized that right quick. I could teach him things and mostly he'd remember. And he still had reason, only it happened to be the reason of a child.

On Fridays it had always been my habit to walk the two miles down to Dehart's Grocery to do my shopping. I could've taken the pickup, and sometimes I did if it was raining or snowing, but mostly I walked. Enjoyed my walks, getting my air. Breathing in the scents of farmhouse lilac in the spring, honeysuckle in summer, fox grapes in fall, wood smoke in winter. Watching the redbuds bloom along the mountainside, telling me another cold winter was behind us, then several months later watch the color slip from the leaves like a bleeding photograph.

Before the accident, Winston had always accompanied me to the store, so I didn't see any reason why things should change afterwards. He'd always loved getting an RC and a sleeve of peanuts before he'd been hurt, and interestingly, the first time we walked into Dehart's after the accident, he went right to the cooler and pulled out a bottle. So some things he still had, but others not so much.

Of course Robert was kind and gentle, with the both of us really. Always had been. That first day when we walked into his store, Robert's eyes moistened up a bit from where he stood behind the counter. And it touched me. Felt my own eyes get a little wet when they met his. Seeing that big, powerful man standing there, knowing that his heart was reaching out to me without saying so much as a word. Robert and I had gone steady back in our school days, and I guess sometimes you can think you've doused a fire, but often there's a few embers that don't quite get put out. But we didn't talk about things like that. He had Ellsabeth, I had Dale, and that was that. But still, seeing him there, the way he reacted, it touched me.

"What do you say there, Winston?" said Robert.

Winston looked at him and said hello right back, just as he always had. But Robert and I shared a quick glance because there was no question that Winston hadn't recognized him. Had no idea at all. And then the eyes really filled up. For both me and Robert. Like I said, some things Winston still had, other things had been wiped out completely. That was the hard part, me having to figure out that fine line.

After our first visit to Dehart's, as we walked along the dirt road on our way home, I stopped Winston when we got to the middle of the old, rickety bridge. I wanted to see if he remembered our ritual. Kind of a test on my part to check his memory. The bridge itself was framed out of iron, but instead of asphalt or concrete, the cross-over was simply railroad ties. In fact, when I walked the fifty yards across it, in a few places there were gaps between the ties where I could actually see the water flowing. The spaces weren't big enough to poke a foot through—most hardly wide enough to slip a quarter through—but there was enough of an opening to get a glimpse of the raging world below. If a car came across, the tires would rattle the ties until I thought the whole thing might collapse.

Years before, during the rains and snowmelt, when the water was really running, Winston and I had stood on that bridge, looking down into the guts of the ravine. That was the first time I explained the significance of the area to him. "We're standing directly over a special spot, Winston. You know why that is?"

"No, ma'am," he'd said as he sipped his RC and stood on tiptoe to look over the railing.

"This is the Eastern Continental Divide you're standing over. Everything in Shooting Creek will one day end up in the Atlantic Ocean, where the sharks will get it. But any streams that flow the other way," I'd said, pointing toward the ridge of mountains to the west, "well, all that water ends up finding the great Mississippi. Go ahead and spit over the side."

Winston had looked at me quizzically but then stretched his toes until his chin rested on the coolness of the railing. He released a thick RC-laden string of saliva and watched as it wiggled and twisted through the air like a snake falling from a tree.

"Do it again," I'd said, laughing.

So Winston spat again.

"Once more."

Winston did it again and laughed with me.

"Thanks to you," I'd said, "the sharks will someday know what RC Cola tastes like." From that day forward, it had become our ritual.

So this time when we stopped—the first time since the accident—I waited anxiously to see what would happen. He put his hands on the rusted I-beam railing and leaned his head over the side. Then he looked up at me, confused, like a puppy seeing itself in a mirror. I didn't do anything except give just the slightest nod of encouragement. I could tell that mind of his was working, trying to figure things out. Could almost hear those gears in his head clicking. He looked down at the water again. And then he spat. I don't think he understood exactly *why* he was spitting, don't think he remembered the story I'd told him, but somewhere deep in his mind there'd been a spark. And a spark was all I'd wanted.

It was right then that my heart about busted. But busted in a good way. He wasn't ever going to be the same, but I knew he was going to be okay. He might have been a little damaged, but he was still my Winston.

Robert

In a community as small as Shooting Creek, it doesn't take long for word to get around. Sometimes it seems like everybody's already heard about something before it even happens. Since most of the gossip takes place either in my store around the stove in winter, or out on the front porch the rest of the year, I generally catch wind before just about anybody. So when something big happened, like Lila Quesenberry's boy nearly getting killed by a horseshoe, well, that really got things riled up.

That particular afternoon, when Lila walked through the screen door, I wasn't exactly sure how to act. I wanted to go right up and hug her, comfort her some, but that just didn't seem appropriate. If anybody'd seen that, the talk would have really started. Word would've gotten ahead to Ellsabeth before I even made it home for the night. Things were shaky enough between me and the wife as it was, so me hugging Lila would've only added fuel to the fire.

Winston still had some bandages on his head, and the left side of his face was bloated and swollen. It appeared soft, as if filled with jelly, and I imagined if I'd poked at it, I would've left a dent, the same as a just hatched chicken egg will do. His eye was partially closed, like he'd started to blink and the lid had forgotten to catch up, with bruising from jaw to hairline. But his other eye was that same bright blue as Lila's. The deep, piercing blue of a jay's feather. I could tell right away he was a little off. Winston had always been as friendly a boy as I'd ever known. Come into the store, all smiles, chattering away. But this time he didn't act like he had the sense to bell a cat.

Lila looked just as pretty as ever though. Her long silver hair pulled into a ponytail, trailing to the middle of her back, brushing against her blouse. She'd started going gray while we were still sweethearts, and since then, her hair had turned a bright silver. Despite that, it somehow didn't make her look old, only wise. It pained me to see her distraught, and I knew that the accident with Winston was only part of the problem. The porch talk had made it common knowledge that Dale had gone back to drinking. There'd been a few times already when I'd wanted to tell some folks to stitch up their mouths and mind their own business, but it would've gotten taken the wrong way. Next thing I would've known, Ellsabeth would've been chastising me about defending Lila's honor. Seems like oftentimes in this life a man can't win for losing.

Sheriff Sutphin

It was early morning when the call came in. Dispatch told me Lila Quesenberry needed an officer out to her place right away. The dispatcher said Lila didn't sound overly fretted, not crying or anything, but she had spoken with urgency. I figured it most likely had something to do with that retarded boy of hers. Probably having a seizure or something.

When I pulled up, it was barely light. Right off I saw the boy over near the chicken coop, bundled in a heavy coat and down on all fours, crawling around and chasing after some loose hens. Little puffs of cold coming from his mouth. From what I'd heard tell of, that was pretty normal behavior now.

As my patrol car crunched the gravel, Lila emerged from the door of the hay barn. That sorry barn looked to be on its last legs, leaning over to one side as if exhausted, the tin roofing lifted up at the edges as if brokeback from seasons of wind. When she popped out, it appeared that a faint fog was following her, creeping out from the door. She was alone, standing there and squeezing her hands together as if wringing out a dish cloth. Just kept doing it, over and over, squeezing one hand and then the other. When she saw me, she gave a wave, but it wasn't a wave of hello. More like, *Come over here. The problem is this way.*

It was only a week before Christmas and bitter cold. If I'd spoken right then, my words would've come out frozen. And even though it was barely light, you could tell it was going to be gray all day. Like the whole world was trapped inside a hornet's nest.

As I approached Lila, my boots crunching the hoarfrost, I noticed she wasn't wearing no coat. Just a nightgown. Figured that's why she worked her hands the way she did, but when I got up next to her she wasn't shivering. It was more like those fidgeting hands were a nervous habit more than anything. Her hair hung down loose over her shoulders, and the silver of it shined despite the ashen morning. And she was pretty in a foreign kind of way. Hadn't really noticed it that first time I'd been there, six months back, but she was. Crystal blue eyes and that silver hair.

"Miss Quesenberry," I said, nodding as I pinched my hat brim.

I think she recognized me, but I saw her glance at the nametag on my coat before she said, "Sheriff Sutphin," and nodded in return.

"What seems to be the trouble?" I said. She didn't appear to be overly out of sorts, but there was something about her—maybe it was those hands—that told me something wasn't right. Or maybe it was just those blue eyes swallowing me up like deep pools of water.

"I guess you ought to see for yourself," she said, motioning toward the barn. She walked and I followed, dropping my boots over the footprints she left in the frost, me watching the faint outline of her thin body beneath that nightgown. "It's Dale," she said, not bothering to look back as she talked. "He's dead."

Lila

Dale had been going out drinking more and more while doing less and less. Shirking his responsibilities and leaving me to feed the chickens, hay the horses, even split stove wood, not to mention seeing after Winston.

He'd never been able to handle his liquor. Right at first, I'd let it go, knowing he felt guilty, but it got to a point where I'd had enough. A person can only take so much. First Winston's accident, then Granddaddy passing a month later, then Dale crawling up inside a bottle every day.

For one thing, he couldn't hardly look at Winston anymore, let alone tend to him. It was like he was allergic. Like Winston was poison ivy. I swear I wondered sometimes if he thought Winston might be contagious.

So it had been some rough going for those past six months. If I'd been a church-type woman, I'd have probably asked the Lord for strength right about then, but I wasn't so I didn't. Instead I confronted Dale one morning at the breakfast table. It was early, still solid black out, the windows covered in crystals around the edges. I didn't know when Dale had come in the night before, but whenever it was, it was well after I'd gone to bed. Shoot, for all I knew, he might've still been up and hadn't even gone to sleep yet. It wasn't like we'd shared a bed in months. Most nights he got liquored up, then fell asleep on the couch by the woodstove.

"It's about time you stopped feeling sorry for yourself and helped me out around here," I said as I picked at my eggs. Even though Dale sat clear across, the stink of last night's whiskey leaked from his skin and churned my stomach. "What's done is done. You need to get sober, pick yourself up, and start back to work. Christmas is eight days off and we need to buy Winston something special."

Dale kept his eyes down, staring at the table. He mumbled under his breath, almost like he didn't want me to hear but speaking just loud enough to make sure that I did. "Ain't like he's gonna appreciate anything we get him anyway. He won't know the difference."

I'd been putting up with his sorry ass for as long as I could stand it. If he wanted to give up on me and stop doing work around the place, if he wanted to mope around and wallow, well, that was one thing. But I wasn't about to let him give up and quit on Winston.

"How in the world do you know what he can and can't appreciate?" I said as I stood up from the table. "How in the world would you know if he can or can't know the difference about anything? It's not like you've been around him for more than a second since you threw a ringer around his god-blessed head. Almost like it was him you were aiming for instead of that post in the sandpit."

Dale pushed his chair away, squeaking the legs across the pine slats. He got up and started for the door, his head hangdog.

"Because if you'd spent even ten minutes with him since you bashed his skull in," I said, my words trailing him, "you'd know that he damn well *can* appreciate things. That he sure as hell *would* know the difference."

At that moment I was like a fiddle string tightened one turn too many. When I heard the truck start up in the barn, I figured he was taking off to somewhere.

Probably down to Dehart's Grocery for a six pack. I imagined him sitting in the parking lot, the heat on full blast as the truck idled, waiting for Robert to open up at five-thirty. What a sorry sight that would've been.

Robert

Word of Dale's death came to the store shortly before noon. It was Scottie Lee Simpkins who came in while several of us was sitting around the potbelly, some sipping on coffee, some taking nips from flasks. In the dead of winter, there wasn't much else to do but huddle up and wait for spring.

Scottie was one of those sorts who always made my stomach drop. Most folks in Shooting Creek were fine and upstanding. Scottie wasn't one of them. He'd been in and out of trouble since he'd been a boy, and whenever he'd come in, my eyes would widen. Had to watch him close or he'd slip something into his pocket, smooth as butter.

He bypassed the circle of us and went straight to the cooler, grabbing a six of High Life bottles. He cracked one, dropping the cap on the floor, and took a long swallow. He reached into the pocket of his grease-smudged work shirt, the sleeves rolled up to his elbows, and pulled out a crumpled pack of smokes. Dark grit was piled underneath his fingernails, his hands and wiry arms smeared with black like he'd been cleaning a chimney.

"Dale Quesenberry died this morning," he said. "Shit,

I was out drinking with him last night. Over at the Pine Tavern. When they closed up, he drove me home. Dropped me off about two-thirty I'd say. We got into a little bottle of busthead, and after we finished it, he left. Next thing I know, the son of a bitch is dead."

Of course that caught our attention. He went through half that six pack as he dragged out the story, making it seem like him and Dale was best buddies when everybody knew Scottie only went around with him because Dale bought him drinks.

While he yammered on, my mind had already switched to Lila. She'd lost her Grandpa Davis a few months back, not to mention Winston's accident, and now this. As horrible as it was, a part of me (and I ain't exactly proud to admit this) was somehow relieved. Lila was available again. I'll probably go straight to hell, but no man can deny his true feelings. And my true feelings had always been with Lila. We'd gotten into an argument shortly after she graduated, broke things off for a little while, and next thing I knew she's marrying Dale. Not a month after we split up. I'd thought it was just temporary. Me being stubborn and not wanting to apologize. Her marrying Dale to spite me. But when she delivered Winston only eight months after they'd married, I knew it wasn't spite that made her do what she did.

By the time I snapped out of my thoughts, Scottie had already slipped out with the rest of the six pack in tow, not having paid me one red cent.

Sheriff Sutphin

"You might want to cover your mouth," she said as I followed her to the barn.

When we got close, I smelled muffler exhaust, the air thick with it. That same gray fog still trickled from the barn, and when I entered, a haze hung inside, collecting in the chestnut rafters.

The pickup door was open, a man slouched inside. A snake of green garden hose went from the tail pipe, over the tailgate, across the bed, and entered the cab through the sliding back window.

"When I got out here," she said, her hand clasping the neck of her nightgown as she pulled it up to mask her face, "I opened the door and turned off the key. I didn't touch anything else, but I already knew it was too late. That's when I went back inside and called."

She told me all of that matter-of-fact. I didn't know if it was the cold, the shock, or what, but she was calm and cool. From outside near the creek, I heard the caw of a crow and the delighted sounds of the boy running around with the chickens. It was an eerie and uncomfortable scene: that retarded boy out there, a silver-haired woman in her nightgown looking at her dead husband, a cloud of exhaust hanging in the cold air, the crow cawing, and it only being a week before Christmas. I couldn't help but feel for Lila right then. The Lord don't put on us more than we can bare, but I thought He was sort of pushing it with her.

Dale sat slumped in the driver's seat, his head leaning

back against the rest, the end of the hose stuck in his mouth like he'd been siphoning gasoline. One eye partially open, staring at the roof. On the seat next to him was a bottle of Jim Beam, uncapped, with just a small taste remaining.

I grabbed Dale's wrist for good measure, but no pulse. His skin was icy, the blood already froze up.

"I'll radio for an ambulance. I sure am sorry."

"Nothing's sacred," she said and walked out.

I scratched a few notes as she yelled for her boy from outside the barn. "Come on, Winston. I got some sausage waiting."

I went to my cruiser and radioed in, then sat in my car to keep warm until they showed up. The morning was light now, still overcast, but I could see well enough. Down in the field across from Shooting Creek was a lone deer at the tree line, foraging before the snow set in. Which got me to thinking. I didn't understand how a man could feel so alone that he'd do that. And not only to himself but to his family. They were the ones had to pick up the pieces, had to continue on. What was it that made a man get so low that he thought sucking down enough exhaust to make his son fatherless and his wife a widow was the best option?

Lila

They say death is a part of life and everything's circular. That couldn't have been more true for me. Seemed like I'd been dealing with death ever since I was born. I don't even remember my mama. She caught pneumonia before I could walk. And I was only seven when Daddy went away. Though I don't remember Mama, I do have memories of Daddy: of times he bought me a Coca-Cola at the general store; of times I sat on his knee and he bounced me as we played Ride-'em-Horsey. But then he was gone. Had been out drinking with his buddies when he got thrown from a car that took a turn too fast.

So I'd seen my fair share. After Daddy passed, I moved in with Granny and Grandpa Davis. Same house I've been raised up in my entire life. Same house I'm still living in now. Over the years I'd learned that death has a way of strengthening a person. Of hardening a person. I'd seen people die all around me, but that didn't mean I was going to give up and rollover like a little pill bug. I knew how to seize an opportunity when it presented itself. If a man decided he wouldn't help me out any longer, if he became worthless, well, I'd find a way to make him worth something. In Dale's case, because of an insurance policy Grandpa Davis gave us after we got married, he turned out to be worth a lot more dead than alive.

It wasn't my fault he'd drunk so much bourbon that he passed out in his truck, not even managing to pull out of the barn. When I still heard the engine grumbling fifteen minutes after he moped from the kitchen that morning, I went to check and see what in the world he was up to. And that's when the opportunity presented itself. There wasn't no planning to it. It just happened.

Seeing that garden hose, all coiled up and resting on a couple of rusty nails tacked to the barn wall, well, it just seemed obvious. I'm not proud of it, necessarily, but I'm not losing sleep either. The fact is, I've got a boy to raise.

Waiting on Joe

Erick, my Lab/Chow mutt, was down at the tree-line chewing on something, content, gnawing and licking the marrow from whatever creature he'd rooted up. On the porch, I attempted to keep my wood shavings in a neat pile as I worked on a replica of Erick, made from a soft chunk of poplar. Wood, it seemed, consumed every aspect of my life. I lived in the woods, I worked on a Christmas tree farm, and during my free time I was either splitting firewood or whittling to avoid the wife.

It had been a tough winter for me and Deborah, cooped up together far longer than was tolerable. She'd been pretty removed lately, and I didn't possess the proper tools to cheer her, neither in my pants nor in my brain. She'd gotten laid-off from her secretary job at the dentist's office (or possibly fired, she'd been a bit murky with the details), so we weren't exactly happy or flush.

I used the tip of my Buck knife to replicate Erick's muscular haunches while the real Erick sprawled in the not-yet-green-grass, still chomping away. That dog was always scavenging, bringing stuff home—woodchucks, squirrels, a three-foot copperhead once. During the spring melt, he'd often drag back field dressings the hunters had left behind, my lawn resembling a full-blown yard sale composed of deer parts.

Inside, Deborah rummaged around, finally awake. She seemed to be sleeping later and later these days, going to bed earlier and earlier. Always on the computer, Facebooking or whatever the hell. Some nights I wanted to climb on the roof and rip down that satellite dish, get rid of our internet, television, the whole goddamned bundle, as it were, toss it in the fucking dumpster. Hard to justify such luxuries when we had bills to pay, groceries to buy. She'd often talked of getting her degree at Community, but I hadn't once seen her make a move in that direction. Come to think of it, the only move I'd seen her make lately was toward another beer. Which made me sick. Only added to the problems. I think it's a weak man (or woman) who uses alcohol to wash away their troubles. Me, well, I never had a taste for it.

My fingers had turned fat and thick from the cold, the unforgiving winter refusing to let go just yet, so my carving was over for the morning. I set my knife and miniature Erick on the table and opened and closed my frozen hands as if casting a spell, attempting to work some blood back in. I whistled for Erick and he popped to attention, his find still stuffed in his jaws.

As he trotted across the yard, wood smoke caught the breeze and trickled down from the chimney, lightly fogging him. Tinges of red shimmered in his black coat when the sun hit it right. He was a tough old bastard. Seventy pounds, solid muscle, total badass. Far as I was concerned, flawless. Deborah felt otherwise.

"He just puked up a baby rabbit on the new rug, Steven," she'd once said. "Jesus Christ, it stinks." And it had stunk, granted, but if a dead rabbit was rotting in *your* gut, you'd probably throw up, too. He was just a dog being a dog, couldn't blame him for that.

He chewed a beer can all to shit one time, which Deborah consequently stepped on, slicing her big toe on the way to the toilet in the middle of the night. He'd puked up plastic Kroger bags on a few occasions. Ate a dirty diaper once. Also an entire junior-sized Wilson leather football. We didn't have kids and I sure as hell had never changed a diaper. Hadn't tossed a ball since grade school. Where he'd found such items was a mystery.

Deborah had issues with Erick, fair enough, but you can't hold a dog accountable for following its instincts. Like now for instance.

As he got closer, I tried to determine what he held so happily. A naked baby doll? The coloring was right. Shoot, he'd found a football once, why not a Barbie? I went to the top stair to greet him, and that's when my heart stuttered. Clamped between his jowls was a human foot, sawed off three inches above the ankle, the skin ragged and jagged as if chewed by some toothy monster. Erick swooshed his tail proudly.

"Shit, Erick," I muttered, glancing behind me. I guess my body language suggested he'd done something wrong because his tail stopped wagging, his head drooped to hangdog. "It's okay, boy," I half-whispered. "Drop it."

He was having none of it. Sensing I was up to something, he tried to make a break for it, unwilling to surrender his trophy. I snatched his collar and grabbed his bottom jaw. "Drop it," I said again, more forcefully. Erick's ears pinned back, his front paws digging in. The foot's stiff toes brushed my wrist which freaked me out. "Motherfucker," I grunted through clenched teeth, realizing my only choice was to grasp that slobber-coated foot like it was Erick's favorite tennis ball. He immediately took it for a game, like a goddamned tug-o-war, and we both pulled and held on with the stubbornness of snapping turtles. But when I said, "*Chase*? You wanna *chase*?" that did the trick and he let go.

He started barking when I didn't hold up my end of the bargain. "Be quiet," I whisper-pleaded, knowing Deborah would open that front door any second now, furious, only to discover me hugging a hairy human foot. I scurried up the steps, grabbed the sports section from a stack of old newspapers, and quickly wrapped that thing as if rolling the world's biggest joint. I twisted the ends, then re-wrapped with the classifieds. Erick was going ape-shit, pissed I'd stolen his treasure.

I held the package tight to my chest, then walked inside and bee-lined for the woodstove. Bacon sizzled in the kitchen, a spatula clinking against a skillet, no doubt Deborah making exactly five pieces for her own self and exactly zero for me, a perfect illustration of where our marriage stood.

"Shut that dog up," she yelled. I envisioned her bleached hair pulled up high on her head in a ponytail as she squinted, a nasty cigarette waggling in her squeezed lips, her face not nearly as pretty as it once was.

"I'll try, dear," I said, stuffing Erick's offering into the coals, using the poker to push it way back. The man's leg hairs ignited and I got a strong whiff before closing the door. Deborah didn't need to know about Erick's discovery. Not just yet. "Sorry. I think he's hungry is all."

"Well, feed him already. Christ, it's too early. I got a ripping headache."

I walked back outside, Erick still yammering about how I'd betrayed him. "Come on, boy," I said, then zipped my jacket snug, grabbed a shovel, headed for the woods. The snow, the ice, it could only keep evil doings hid for so long. "*Hike,* boy? Wanna go for a *hike?*"

It was a pretty sorry excuse for a grave. But when dug in haste, and with fatigue setting in after sawing and digging and lugging and burying, a bit of slack had to be extended when it came to the particulars.

Erick had really gone to town—dirt scattered every which way, dead leaves strewn about like feathers from a slaughtered goose. The only body part I saw was a leg wearing a scrap of blue jean, and that was enough for me; no reason to delve deeper. Wasn't like I needed to confirm his face; I knew good and well who he was. I hoped Erick hadn't already carried off the head or arms or whatever, leaving bits of the man scattered about like a trail of breadcrumbs.

Erick had led me right to the plot using an established

deer path that meandered through oaks and rhododendron thickets. It was also a path that, if followed for
another half mile, would've taken me straight to Willie
Koonz's back door. Willie, as it so happened, was the
man currently half-buried in the soil. He had two kids
and a wife, them wondering where he'd run off to three
months prior. He'd been my supervisor. The guy I'd
worked with on the tree farm for five years. He was also
the guy who'd been fucking my wife for the past eight
months before he disappeared, sneaking through these
very woods, on this very deer path, during lunch hour.
Supposedly he went home to eat during our break while
me and the Mexicans stayed in the fields, our boots
dangling over pickup tailgates, me eating partially frozen
peanut butter and jelly sandwiches, them gorging on
still-hot tamales wrapped tightly in corn husks that their
pretty wives—with skin like warm honey—had, earlier
that morning, cooked and sealed in foil, which in turn
always made me envious but I never had the gumption
to ask if maybe (just once) they'd bring an extra for me,
them probably thinking I was pleased as punch with the
cold, stale *gringo* sandwiches I slapped together every
morning because my wife, sure as shit, didn't make them
for me, her still sleeping away, waiting for lunchtime so
my boss could come over and give her the business in my
own bed while my bony ass turned numb on the freezing
metal ridges of that aforementioned tailgate.

So, yeah, there was that.

I'd figured out the affair a year back. The Mexicans
were doing the season's first mowing while me and

Willie planted seedlings on a hillside. Squatting, kneeling, digging little holes, dropping in trees no higher than a hand. Long, sunny days but not so damn hot like it would be in another month when we'd be culling dead trees, the son-of-a-bitching yellow jackets in the ground, lying in wait for you to step on their nests, or the hornets in their paper globes tucked in the trees, praying you'd slice into their hive with your trimming machete so they could zoom out like a squadron of fighter jets, just for the fun of it. But in March and April, things were still pleasant. The magenta of redbuds dotting the mountainsides, the white of dogwoods. Oaks dropping their tassels from the sky like heavenly pipe cleaners.

When it's just you and one other guy, and that guy's come back from lunch, and he smells strangely familiar, in fact, smells not only like that perfume your wife insists on—which she can only find at select TJ Maxx stores—but also like the unmistakable sweaty sex of her puss, well, you start to wonder. Then, when the breeze shifts, and Willie is upwind of you, and suddenly Deborah's fragrance filters down the slope and your nose starts twitching the same as Erick's when he whiffs an injured bunny rabbit, well, your brain starts connecting the dots, puts the pieces together. A man knows his wife's odor, that's all I'm saying.

That, in and of itself, wasn't enough proof. Hell, maybe Willie's wife smelled similar. I mean, maybe it's like snowflakes. Every one of them's different, but from a distance they all appear pretty damn equal. So it's not out of the realm of possibility that Deborah and Willie's wife could've had a nearly identical odor. They live within a mile of each other, probably our wells are tapped into the same aquifer—pardon the expression—so maybe it's in the water. Who's to say? All I know is when that pleasant breeze drifted down the hillside, there was no doubt Deborah's unique and particular aroma floated on that stream of lazy, warm air.

A few weeks later, me and Willie are fertilizing when he gets to ripping on me. He was always bullying, but that day it was with more *oomph*. "Don't you got goals, Steve? What're you doing with your life?"

I hated when people called me Steve. My name's Steven, I always introduced myself as such, and I'd corrected Willie many times. "Doing about the same as you," I said. "We're both dipping our hands into dried-up horseshit which, by some weird-ass miracle, makes trees grow."

"Yeah, but this is temporary for me," he said. "I got bigger plans."

"Five years on the job doesn't sound very temporary, Willie. Five years sounds pretty permanent."

He spit, wiping tobacco trickle into his beard. "I've got some stuff on the side," he said. "Me and my brother, we been investing in shit. You ever heard of semi-conductors?"

"Like a part-time orchestra leader?" I said, messing with him. If there was one thing I knew, it was technology. I only had a high school diploma, but I was always playing with electronics, tinkering. Probably had the fastest Wi-Fi connection in the county, not that Deborah appreciated it. Something I'd learned over the years was that people generally thought I was stupid. No matter, because I'd found it to be an asset. When people assume you're dumb, they let down their guard.

"I don't know how they work," he said, "but Barth says it's related to cell phones. We've been dumping money into this company he knows of, got an inside tip, and it's about to hit big. That's what I mean, Steve. I got plans, man, more than baling and loading fucking Christmas trees the rest of my life."

"Semi-conductors, huh? Like you talking about core cooling capacitors, that type of shit?" I was that kid you probably went to school with, the one always tearing apart radios, TVs, just to see how they worked, then putting them back together.

"Speak English, man. I swear you're worse than them goddamn wetbacks half the time. I don't know what the fuck you just said. Anyway, you need to think bigger." Willie reached into his fertilizer bag and tossed a handful around the base of a Frazier fir. "Stop acting like an idiot, wasting your time carving stupid shit out of wood. You need to plan for your future."

"Hmm, maybe so," I said. And I did start planning, right then, because I'd never discussed my whittling with him. In fact, I'd never mentioned it to anyone, other than Deb obviously. It was private, just something I did. And me and Willie, we didn't mingle outside of work. When we'd first met, there'd been discussions of us and the wives getting together to grill burgers, the way new acquaintances will do, imagining they've found that perfect match where the wives have everything in common, scrapbooking and collecting Longaberger baskets or Beanie Babies, and the guys love bow hunting and Earnhardt—but that never panned out. So there was no way he could've known about me carving "stupid shit out of wood" unless he'd been to my house. Not just *to* my house, but *inside,* and not just inside, but all the way back to my bedroom where I kept my finished pieces on a dresser, mostly of Erick in various states of repose. So that, along with the stink of my wife on his clothes, well, that got me to planning for my future all right.

"You ever seen *Risky Business?*" continued Willie, chuckling. "God, what a great movie. 'Sometimes you just gotta say *What the fuck,* Steve.' Best line ever."

A stripe of spittle dripped from his beard like lace from a spider's ass, and I considered countering with a quote of my own, lifted from a fortune cookie I'd once cracked open. "Live life like a mighty river." I loved that. I was a mighty river, ready to unleash my power. But in my own way, on my own terms.

It was me who'd first discovered how bad off Joe actually was. I was late for work, zipping my old Charger tight around a corner, when I nearly hit him as he walked the road's edge, gimping along. I braked, rolled down the passenger window. "What do you know good, old man?" I said. He caught my eye, then kept on.

I nudged the car forward. "Jump in, Joe, before you get killed. Where you heading?"

He glanced over but didn't stop. "Gotta see the doc. Alternator belt's shot on my truck."

"The doctor? In town? That's ten miles. Get your ass in here before I jump out and stuff you in."

"You wrassle with a rattlesnake, you bound to get bit," he said, taking a long, deep draw from his cigarette. Deborah had gotten her orneriness honestly, that's for sure, but he did concede, opened the door, started to enter.

"Whoa, hold up," I said, raising my free hand. "You can't smoke in here."

Joe stopped midstream, tightened his jaw, began walking again, not bothering to close my door. "Go piss your pants, you son of a bitch."

"Shit," I muttered, inching the car forward, careful not to slap his ass with the open door. I leaned across the huge front seat, yelled to him. "C'mon, I'm sorry. Finish up and get in."

He kept walking, ignoring me, but I wouldn't relent. Finally he flicked his cigarette into the broom sedge and entered, the whole process a struggle as he twisted that twisted body into the front seat. His chest heaved in small spurts.

"You really need to quit smoking, Joe."

"Just drive, peckerhead." He stared at me, his eyes as hard and dark as the coal he'd extracted from the ground for fifty years.

I liked Joe well enough. Grouchy old thing, tough as

leather plow line, his body bent and mangled like a crashed car, but he always told it straight.

"What're you going in for?" I asked.

"Cain't breathe, Steve," he said, lighting a fresh cigarette. "Reckon doc's gonna tell me for certain what I already been knowing for years."

So it was me who'd been with Joe when he'd received the official news, only a month after I'd learned his daughter was screwing Willie. He had the black lung—which might sound horrible—but for a retired coal miner, it meant a check he could live out his days on, something to leave for his family.

The doctor brought in X-rays, clamped them to the backlit screen. Joe hadn't wanted me in there, had said, "Get on to work before I slit your throat," but his rheumy eyes said something different. So I insisted, ignored his objections. Those X-rays looked like some foreign black universe with a splattering of white stars. Each star, explained the doc, was coal dust, scarring the lungs. Joe didn't ask questions, just gazed ahead, absorbing it as if he'd known since boyhood this day was inevitable. He'd left school in eighth grade to enter the mines, only exited a few years back. That was the shit of it all. Work fifty years underground just to be put back in it permanently, right when you'd finally come up for air. As if day-by-day, year-by-year, all you'd been doing was digging your own grave.

That was his life. Mines every day, a wife, two kids—

Deborah, of course, and her older brother, Russ, who'd made it to eleventh grade before going underground, only to be blown up ten years back. After the explosion, with his son dead, with his wife gone many years before, Joe moved from the little mining town of Grundy—the only home he'd ever known—to a singlewide in the Blue Ridge to be closer to his daughter, for whatever that was worth. No love lost between those two. Saw each other maybe three times a year. It was me who often checked on him, made sure he was getting by all right, especially after the diagnosis.

It was also me who'd helped Joe get his tanks in order. At first, those clear plastic tubes jammed up his nose drove him bat-shit. He'd hobble around, bitching, pulling his little cart behind him like a pissed off caddy, the thin blue oxygen tank his golf clubs. Once a month, I'd go over to Radford to the gas place for refills. As teenagers, we used to hop their chain-link fence at night and steal tanks of nitrous oxide, then buy big punching balloons at the pharmacy, fill them, have insane parties, everybody so fucked up they'd stumble, fall, and some-times convulse. The gas people eventually got wise—installed hurricane wire, locked the nitrous in a cage—but did we ever fry some brain cells for a while, our entire class whacked on dental grade laughing gas most of senior year. Man, I'd changed a lot since then.

Several weeks after I determined Deborah was knocking boots with Willie, I drove to Crosshairs, the local hunting outfitter, to make a purchase. Not for a gun, but instead for a couple of trail cameras—the ones with motion sensors so hunters can discover what monster bucks roam their forests. Simple setup, really. I put one above the floodlight spotting the driveway and another in a tree along that trail leading to Willie's.

That following Monday, after Deborah was asleep, I checked the computer to confirm my suspicions. Sure enough, during lunch while I sat with the Mexicans, me fantasizing about their young, dark-skinned wives, guess who appeared on my trail cam software? That cock-sucker, Willie, that's who, sneaking through the woods. Then the house camera picked him up, strutting along my driveway, cool as a goddamn cucumber.

The same deal unfolded for the next several months. I stewed so bad I couldn't stand it. Not so much because I gave a hell about Deborah anymore or felt betrayed by my coworker who had the balls to stick it to my wife nearly every day, then return to work an hour later and tell me my tree trimming was a bit sloppy, but more because I was scared Deb might file for divorce. Which wasn't an option. Not yet. That didn't jive with my financial plans. But a man can only take so much. So I decided if they liked games, I'd play a few of my own. Mess with their tiny brains a bit.

Once, when I'd mentioned that Joe was a good man, Deborah had gone off. "Don't you dare. You don't know a goddamn thing about it." I'd assumed this meant Joe used to be rough on her as a child, maybe knocked her around a bit, but I was wrong. "He was a drunk. A real bastard. I don't think he remembered my name most days."

"Coal mining's a tough job. He probably—"

"Don't you dare defend him, Steven. You want an example of what a *good man* he was?"

I shrugged. "Sure, why not?"

"He used to go to the shelter and get cats, pretend he was adopting them, okay? Once home, he'd break their legs with a hammer, leave 'em mewing in the barn. Those cries still keep me up some nights. Then in the evenings, he'd sit in the loft drinking beer, waiting to shoot the curious coyotes who wandered in. For the bounty."

"Well, it *was* just cats. And son-of-a-bitching coyotes. Not like it was dogs or cattle or something."

"That's awful, Steven. Cats are God's creatures, same as dogs."

"I'll tell you right now, cats sure as shit *aren't* the same as dogs. Not even fucking close."

"Doesn't mean they should be abused."

"That's not what I meant. Shit, they were gonna die at that shelter anyway."

"You're disgusting. God loves all His miracles equally."

All I can say is she never showed that sort of compassion toward Erick. Not once. And okay, fair enough, no animal should be abused—not even cats, I guess. But oh, Jesus, did it make me crazy when she preached her

Bible bullshit. Full-on hypocrite. Prime example? When I'd gotten home from Joe's first doctor's visit and advised her of his prognosis, she'd said, "Hallelujah. About time."

What she meant, of course, was that the diagnosis equaled compensation. Money that would set us up good once Joe died. Her brother was dead from the mines, her mother a suicide—slit her wrists in a bathtub; Deborah found her when she'd gotten home from school, only a freshman—so Deborah was the sole heir. Wouldn't get rich, but between that and the settlement from Russ's death in the mine collapse, we'd be doing okay for a while.

So I had no interest in divorce. Last thing I wanted was for Willie to somehow get his hands on even one dime of that money. I needed to break them up.

Out in the fields, I put my sabotage plan in motion. Started dropping hints. "But it's weird, Willie. I mean, me and Deborah, well, we haven't exactly been frisky in months. So if she really is pregnant...shoot, I don't know what's going on." The way Willie shifted, the way he nervously passed that trimming machete from one hand to the other, man, it was priceless.

Toying with Deborah was even more fun, and one evening while eating dinner, I laid it on thick. Vanna was on the tube pushing letters as we sat in the living room, shoveling in peas and potatoes from our potpies. I had a lemonade, she one of those Redd's Apple Ale things that'd been on the commercials lately.

"So I was talking with Willie today," I said, "and you know what he told me? He's a real jackass, that guy." I paused, all cool like. Wanted to watch her squirm. But she was staring at that screen, only one blank left in the entire puzzle: THE P_INTED DESERT. She shouted at the TV, "*The Pointed Desert*, you dumb shit," just as the contestant on *Wheel* said the same exact thing (I swear to God) minus the "dumb shit" part. Sajak said, "No, I'm sorry, but you still have time." The guy sounded things out, repeated "*The Pointed Desert*" and Sajak, super-cool as always, replied, "No matter how many times you say it, the puzzle's not going to change." Deborah said, "What the hell?" so I chimed in, "The *Painted* Desert," which of course was the correct answer and what the next contestant said. The woman got twenty-five hundred bucks for her winning efforts. I got *nada*. "Did you hear me?" I said. "About Willie?"

"What? No," she snapped, staring down the television as if somehow betrayed. Like Sajak and company were running a conspiracy. "What happened?"

"Willie said something today I couldn't believe. Said he was stepping out on his wife."

She lifted her bottle, paused mid-raise, wouldn't look at me. "Huh, well, I guess there's trouble in paradise."

"Not according to him. Says he's just got another girl he likes better. Wants to be with."

Did she half-smile as she took a sip of Redd's? Possibly.

"Shit happens all the time, right?" she said, cutting

some potpie crust with her fork and stuffing it in, grinning like a wolf.

"I don't know, just seems lowdown. Blindsiding his wife like that. Two kids and all. I mean, if it was you and me, I'd just tell you."

"Yeah."

"And you'd do the same, right? No behind the back stuff?"

"Yeah," she repeated, her eyes locked on the television, staring at that new creepy Colonel Sanders as he peddled chicken, her seeming to only half-pay attention to me. But I assure you, I had her ear.

"He said he hooked up with that cute little thing down at the Tavern. You know, that new blonde who waits tables?"

Her head whipped in my direction. "With *who*?"

"That woman—hell, *girl* really—at the Tavern. Melody, I think her name is. Short skirts, legs to here," I said, raising my hand well above my head. This was fun.

Her lips pursed.

"Said they're going to take off on Saturday. His wife and kids are out of town, visiting her mother and he's running away to Myrtle Beach. Leaving a note, and *poof*, just like that, he's gone. Crazy, huh?"

That bit about his wife going out of town was the only true part, by the way, Willie having mentioned it at work. You sprinkle in a few truths with your lies and people eat it up.

Deborah looked at Vanna, back from commercial. "Yeah, I reckon so."

"Good news for us is I'll get the foreman job. A few more bucks. Mr. Majors ain't gonna give it to no Mexican."

She grabbed her plate and walked toward the kitchen, her face blank. If I could've magically pried open the top of her head right then, I'd've seen those gears whirring at double-time, grinding like an unoiled machine, smoke pouring from the works.

The day after I'd messed with Deborah, something curious happened: Willie failed to return to work after lunch. That son of a bitch was a lot of things, but unreliable wasn't one of them. That evening I checked my trail cam software, and sure enough, he'd headed toward my house that afternoon, sneaking through the woods like a horny tomcat. But the footage never showed him leaving. What it did capture, however, precisely an hour and twenty-three minutes later, according to the timestamp, was Deborah passing by, pushing my wheelbarrow, which in all my days I'd never seen her do. Far as I knew, that woman didn't know which end of a hammer to hold. But as usual, I'd underestimated her. She was full of surprises.

Days and weeks later, small town details funneled through the rumor mill. One in particular was that Willie had left a note stating he was leaving his family. Nobody seemed too surprised by this, least of all his wife. She never even bothered to call the cops when she got back from her weekend at her mother's, just assumed the no good scoundrel had left her high and dry. Which turned out to be particularly good fortune for me and Deborah.

I didn't let on to Deborah that I knew anything about what she'd done. I had my reasons for keeping quiet. But it was weird, living in that house with her afterward, realizing what she was capable of. I'd find myself looking at her from across the table every once in a while, thinking, Man, *that's one wicked-assed woman.* But she was cool. You'd never guess, not in a million years, she'd sawed up her lover and buried him in the woods.

"I'm leaving you," said Deborah. This was three weeks after Erick had brought me the foot, several months since Willie had gone missing. I have no idea why it took her so long to make that decision, but I'm assuming she wanted to be sure the smoke had cleared.

"No," I said. "No, you're not."

"Bite me, Steven. I'll do whatever I damn well please."

"Mmm, no you won't." That's when I got off the couch and approached the front door—all smooth and cavalier, like I had all the power, all the answers—and ran my hand along the casing. "Let me show you something, Deb. I'm figuring you plugged these with chewing gum?" I said when my fingers located the first of the three patched bullet holes, almost like I was reading Braille. "Then smeared them with shoe polish?" I rubbed both my pointer and middle finger against my thumb, as if demonstrating the universal "money" sign, while showing her the inky residue. "Pretty good match, really. I'm impressed."

"Listen, baby, you got things a little mixed up," she said, playing it cool but unable to hide her panic. Plain as day, I saw her envisioning where exactly my rifle was at that moment. Saw her calculating speed and time and distance to the closet, figuring whether she could race to it before I tackled her. Of course it didn't matter, since I'd already moved the gun. And unloaded it.

"I don't have a thing mixed up, Deborah. In fact, it's all clear as day."

"I don't know what you're talking about. I didn't do nothing."

That's when I popped in the flash drive, played the video. She stood over my shoulder and watched her own self, right there on the computer screen, all bloody and goopy, pushing body parts down the trail. Three separate trips. It was almost funny, in a sick, demented sort of way, I admit, but it was humorous watching Erick follow at her heels as she struggled with that wheelbarrow, strong-arming it down the trail. Even when she halted and clearly yelled at him, presumably ordering him back to the house, his tail just slapped back-and-forth like a windshield wiper. He ignored her completely.

One particular part of the video seemed to really unsettle her. Of Willie's head bouncing up and out of the barrow when the wheel clipped a rock, then rolling along the trail for a few feet like a kid's wayward ball. I glanced back to see her nose crinkle as she relived that scene: her scooting around the wheelbarrow, picking up his head, plopping it back in as if harvesting pumpkins. She could've closed her eyes as the video played, could've turned away or walked off, but she watched intently. Instead of being unsettled, as I'd first assumed, I realized she seemed almost fascinated. Suddenly it was me who felt uneasy.

"It's also saved to a second jump drive," I explained, "and stored in a safe place with instructions. Thought you should know, just in case you're considering cutting me up into bits like your boyfriend."

"Steven, you don't understand. There's—"

"I figured out most of it, Deb. Though, I confess, I still don't know how you forced him to write a note. You're good, I'll give you that. Damn smart."

And that, right there—along with the video—was the key to her spilling everything. Simple flattery. Who'd've thunk it? Offer her a little praise about a cold-blooded murder she'd committed, and boy, she ate it up. Actually chuckled. "He didn't write a note."

"He didn't?"

"I did."

"You?"

"He denied everything. Said there wasn't no other woman. Got all emotional, started boo-hooing, though I reckon a gun pointed straight at your chest has a way of doing that. Him crying got me all fired-up and flustered. Then *bam bam bam,* and he's dead on the floor. I barely touched that trigger. Didn't even mean to do it.

"When I'm burying him, I find a receipt in his pocket. From the XPress Mart, right? Had his fingerprints on it, which got me to thinking. I walk to his house when I'm done, let myself in with his keys, scratch a note on the back of it. Simple block lettering. He wrote like a third grader, so it was easy."

I rubbed my whiskers, cupped my chin. "Pretty damn good, Deb. I gotta give credit where credit's due." Figured I'd keep buttering her up, see what other info I might squeeze.

She grinned wide and lit a smoke. I'd never seen her so proud. "Stashed his truck at Daddy's."

She was gushing now. Who was I to stop her? "So Joe knows?" I said.

"Knows enough not to ask questions. So like I said, I'm leaving."

I shook my head. "And like *I* said, no, you're not."

"What the hell, Steven? We're done. You know it, I know it. No reason to stick around, so don't play me."

"You and me, we're gonna sit tight, happy and hunky-dory. And wait."

"What do you mean 'wait'?"

"On Joe."

"On Daddy? Wait for goddamn what, goddamnit?" Her eyes darted, searching for her smokes even though one still smoldered between her fingers.

"Wait on him to croak. Doc says he's got a year left, max, probably only six months. Once I get my half, you're free to roll. But until then, you're staying right by my side. For better or worse, remember?"

"You ain't getting half," she said, but the statement lacked conviction. She knew she was beat.

"I'm going out on the porch for the sunset," I said. "Give you a little time to ponder, maybe re-watch that video if you want. Think about what the cops might say if they got their hands on it somehow."

Thirty minutes later, she joined me, a fresh smoke pinched in her fingers. Erick sat between my knees, getting his ears rubbed.

"I been thinking," she said.

"Uh-huh."

"I don't wanna wait."

"Well, Deb, in this particular instance, I'd say you don't got much choice."

It appeared she hadn't heard me. "You know, lately I've noticed Daddy's been down in the dumps. Suicidal even. Maybe I should call his doctor, tell him I'm worried about his mental status or whatever."

"Stability?"

"Yeah, that." She paused as if waiting for me to fully comprehend her meaning. Her intentions. Like she was giving me a second to let it all sink in.

"Deb, it's only six months. Year at the most. Not long in the whole scheme of things."

"Or better yet," she continued, "what if them oxygen tubes accidentally got pinched under a table leg or something?"

"Jesus, Deb."

"Oh, Jesus yourself, Steven. Fuck Jesus."

I once again found myself fearful, and slightly in awe, of my wife. But if truth be told, it was exactly what I'd been expecting. And hoping for.

"You're a dark, dark woman, Deb."

She remained quiet, deep in thought. The only sound on the porch was the shuffle of her bare feet as she paced, and the faint crackle of cigarette paper, that cherry burning hot as it raced down the shaft on her inhale. She shot me a nasty look, but her expression softened when she saw my own. Maybe it was the way my mouth had turned up at the corners, not quite a smile, exactly, but something close. Or maybe it was my eyes, the way I imagined they glimmered as the evening sun lit them up just before vanishing behind the distant hills. Like we were communicating without saying a word.

"I've never been able to change your mind, once it's set on something," I said, feeding her fire. "Like a bulldog, you are."

"Damn straight," she said, looking confident as she stared off at the shotgunned sky, a spattering of purples and oranges and blues.

I gave Erick a good rub on his head, realizing I might not have to wait on Joe nearly as long as I'd first thought. And that pleased me to no end. Pleased me real good.

The Pawn

Henry's pale skin burned. He hadn't eaten in five days. Hadn't slept in three. Not one wink. And other than the fishing rod in his hand and the tackle box next to him in the dirt, he'd pawned everything he owned. Everything. When Jad, his oldest buddy from high school, had kicked him out that morning, Henry had nowhere else to go, so he grabbed his fishing gear and hitchhiked down to the river. And that's where he sat now, on a rotting sycamore log, his sneaker nudging at a faded and cracked night crawler cup.

"That's it, man," Jad had said a few hours earlier. "Get out. You can't crash here anymore. You haven't paid me shit in two weeks."

Henry hadn't protested. The only thing he said, after he grabbed his rod from the corner of the trailer's living room, was, "Can you hook me with a few bucks for a bag? I'll pay you as soon I get some cash. I got a hundred coming from Jackhammer soon."

"Look in a mirror and tell me if you need another bag."

And Henry did just that. He went into the bathroom (carrying his rod, paranoid Jad might steal it otherwise) and took a piss. After zipping up, the mirror showed someone he didn't recognize. A face turned the gray of fuzzy vegetable mold, the upper parts of both cheeks scabbed and pocked. Several teeth had fallen out, and the ones that remained were yellowed and rotting. And his eyes...he refused to make eye contact with himself. That's how bad it'd gotten.

He left the bathroom and mumbled to Jad, "Yeah, I think I need another bag. Just one to get me through."

"Jesus, you gotta go. You're totally whacked."

"Just a few bucks. Come on, man, please."

"Get out, Henry," said Jad as he clamped onto a mop handle, wielding it like an axe.

Henry left the trailer, walked the dirt driveway, and eventually caught a ride from the owner of a junkyard flatbed, en route to a smashed Subaru down by the river. When the guy dropped him off at the railroad crossing, Henry nodded thanks, then headed over the rough gravel along the tracks, checking his back pocket every five seconds, ensuring that the Marlboros he'd swiped off the seat hadn't somehow jumped out and run away.

After rigging his pole with a frog-patterned Jitterbug, Henry lit a cigarette. The book of matches only had three remaining, so he built a fire before casting. Though the early morning August sun already penetrated the wide expanse of the New River, he had gone into survival mode. He had a full pack of smokes and only three matches. Unless he wanted to jumpstart a new cigarette before the previous one burned out, he had to plan ahead.

Between the sun burning his skin, and the fire's heat on his back, Henry knew he should be perspiring. But there was nothing left in his body to sweat out. And every time a tiny drop beaded on his forehead, he swiped it with his finger and sucked, hoping for a few residual traces of crystal.

He tried to figure how long since he'd snorted the last of it, but he'd lost track of time weeks ago. He knew he'd been at Jad's, it was dark outside—he did recall that—and he'd been staring at the TV, but at what show, he had no idea. Now, the pounding in his head warned that he needed more, and quickly. He checked every pocket of his jeans several times over, but there was none to be had.

And then the voices started. He'd heard them a few times before, and with each occurrence, he'd walked to the pawnshop to part with another piece of his life: his stereo; the rifle his father had forgotten when he walked out on Henry and his mother years earlier; the antique Bowie knife from his grandfather. All he had now was the fishing rod and a tackle box stuffed with rusty-hooked lures. He knew the bastard at the pawn shop wouldn't give him shit for it.

So the voices began, softly at first, but getting louder until they screamed and shrieked with such intensity that Henry wanted to split his head open with a rock and strangle the voices within. He picked his nose and sucked off anything that clung to his fingers. Mostly it was the black crusts of dried blood, but he ate it anyway, imagining a faint burn on his tongue from the bitter chemical. He pushed his thumbs deep against his eyelids, relieving pressure. He made fists and knuckled them against his temples.

At the edge of the river, he cupped his hands and drank, watching a crawdad propel itself backwards under a rock. A few copper minnows glimmered in a beam of sunlight and stared at him with blank, stupid looks, the way fish will do. They mocked him. "Look at you," they said. "Nothing but a junkie." And then they darted away, laughing, when Henry angrily smacked the surface.

He lit a cigarette using a flimsy twig from the fire, then sat on a log and grabbed his fishing rod, convinced that the water had done the trick. The voices had subsided, at least momentarily.

But the screeches began again, though different this time: metal on metal, distant at first, but steadily growing louder. It was only when he turned away from the glass of the river that he saw the coal train, the cars flickering through the tree trunks like strobe lights. But as the rhythmic clicking whooshed by—only fifty yards from Henry—he realized that the craving, the yearning for the crystal, had indeed subsided. When the rear engine pushed the rest of the cars past, and the hum was swallowed by the mountains, Henry tossed his butt into the fire and closed his eyes.

* * *

The sun awakened him. He was stretched out on a bed of cool dirt near the riverbank, a faint hint of wood-smoke creeping into his burned-out nostrils. He struggled to get upright, brushed off the needles and debris, and looked at the sun, low in the sky. He didn't know if it was morning or evening. Birds chirped from the surrounding trees, and a pair of squirrels played tag in the sprawling branches of an oak.

He examined the blackened remains of his campfire. With a stick, he poked at the ashes, finding a few embers barely clinging to life. He dropped some pine needles and dead leaves on the coals, and blew with a smooth, methodical breath, the way his grandfather had taught him. As the flames caught, he added more twigs, then thicker sticks.

Other than the bird twitters and a subtle *flit-flit* as the fire worked the branches, the surrounding forest was silent. The smoke climbed vertically toward the sky in a tight, organized column. Everything was calm, the river hardly flowing. Henry determined it to be morning, that he'd slept all night, and confirmed it shortly thereafter, noticing the sun slightly higher above the tree-line.

He settled himself on a log, lit a cigarette. The softness of the morning light comforted him. The faint wisps of river fog, like translucent wraiths, floated and burned away as the sun worked its magic. A shaft of orange light stretched across the New's expanse and lit up a hula-hoop patch of water directly in front of him. The circle clearly exposed everything—another entire world existing below. Gold flecks sparkled in frozen suspension, bits of leaves and other organic debris turned in slow motion; a caddis fly rose to the surface, creating microscopic ripples as it furiously attempted to dry its wings. After a moment's struggle, the little insect fluttered away, rising higher and higher until it disappeared.

And then, as if synchronized by a symphony conductor, thousands of caddis flies hovered over the river, greenish-white clouds appearing where only seconds before there'd been nothing. Suddenly, the conductor instructed the symbols to crash; the water boiled as fish began feeding. Henry watched the performance with fascination.

Fascinated, that is, until his head snapped and buzzed. The voices started, though not nearly as intense as the previous day. Henry grabbed a handful of damp stones from the river's edge and flung them, one by one, but they were clunky and didn't skip well. So instead, he plopped them into the circle of light while fighting the ripping in his head. The stones squiggled and darted, appearing drunk—if rocks could appear drunk.

A distant train whistle awoke him from his trance. He realized he'd again fought through the voices. As he looked at the tracks, awaiting the engine's approach, something flickered in his periphery. He zeroed-in, locating a doe in the shadows, her brown tail occasionally twitching, exposing glimpses of white. Her head was bowed as she foraged. Henry clicked with his cheek and she sprang to attention, head cocked, neck extended.

She saw him but wasn't alarmed. Henry stayed perfectly still, admiring her grace as she stepped closer to the track embankment and resumed eating.

Henry fed the fire but never lost the deer. The metallic rumble of the train increased. Suddenly he realized that on either side of the doe, not more than four feet away, were two more deer, also rummaging along the forest floor. They had materialized out of nowhere.

The train whistled again, this time much louder, and the clicking along the tracks began its hypnotic beat. Two of the deer, including the one Henry had first spotted, propped their heads to attention, but the third continued eating. As the metronomic hum got louder, the two alert deer effortlessly bounded up the small hill and over the tracks to the other side.

To his left, the engine turned the corner as the headlight peeked through the trees a hundred yards away. When he looked back to the third doe, she was no longer there. Across the tracks, the other two were motionless, staring in Henry's direction. And then, just a bit farther down, he spotted the solitary doe, standing in the middle of the tracks, her head bent and foraging between the crossties, but for what, Henry couldn't imagine. He glanced to the train as it drew dangerously near, then back to the vulnerable deer, and repeated as if watching a tennis match. Henry waved his arms. "Get off the tracks. What the hell're you doing? Are you deaf? Get off the tracks."

As the engine screamed, the doe remained stationary. She finally looked up, but the train was already on top of her. The engine skewed Henry's sight, so he didn't see the impact, but he felt just as sick as if he had. He couldn't do anything except watch while car after car flashed by. He ran toward the foot of the hill, waiting futilely as the endless line rolled on. Brown painted steel, crested with mounds of chunked coal, whipped past. The wind stung his face. *Norfolk & Southern* was stamped into the sides of every car, presumably heading toward Virginia Beach or somewhere along the coast. When the rear pusher engine finally passed and the train disappeared into the mountains, Henry searched the vacant and lonely strip of track. Everything had gone hauntingly quiet. No sign of the doe, no mangled pieces, no destroyed and bloody carcass. Across the tracks, the other two deer, now slightly farther up the mountainside, fed once more, their tails casually twitching.

Henry climbed the embankment and stood on the ties, the thick, sweet smell of creosote filling his damaged nose. Patches of black tar cooked in the heat. The silver steel rails gleamed. Just on the other side, in the bottom along the gravel and rocks, he saw the third deer— standing, her head upright, her tail hanging down, perfectly content.

The doe casually strode toward her companions, in no hurry. When they'd regrouped, they trekked up the sharp mountainside together as quietly as owls on the wing, then melted into the landscape. Henry wondered if the doe understood how dangerously close she'd been.

Henry soaked up the beauty surrounding him: the lush Virginia mountains; the cobalt sky sprayed with white cumulus clouds; the river's glimmer below; his little fire sending off a gray stream through the trees. He felt alive.

He spied a huge thicket of blackberry bushes running along the tracks. For the first time in many days, hunger tugged at him. He dropped into the bottom, spilling a cascade of gravel down the embankment, and immediately popped the purplish-black fruit into his mouth. The sweet-sour juice trickled from his lips and down his chin as he voraciously picked and stuffed, picked and stuffed. He ate like a feral dog. He ate like a man who hadn't ingested anything but pure chemical for a week.

When he returned to the fire, he picked tiny seeds from his teeth, then went for a drink. His fingers were stained a deep purple as he cupped them to the river, so he scrubbed with pebbles. Then he removed his clothing and waded in, plopping sand in his hair, massaging it into his scalp. A coarse rock from the bottom became his washcloth. As he scoured, bits of old, gray skin fell to the surface like snow, mingling with the transparent exuviae of the caddis flies.

Afterwards, standing by the fire, he decided he'd finally cast his rod. Childlike excitement grew with the anticipation of catching a fish, something he hadn't experienced in years. But this time the voices didn't come softly; they returned with abandon, raging violently. Blood throbbed along his temples, pain pierced every recess of his skull. He thought he might vomit. He dropped his cigarette and tried to drink water, but his hands shook so violently that he couldn't manage a sip.

Visions of his screaming father told him what a no good son-of-a-whore he was. He opened his eyes to remove the images, but they refused to go away. He closed his eyes, but they persisted. Using the heels of his hands, he ground them into his eye sockets, slightly relieving the pressure, but he was sick. He needed a hit. He had to have a bump of crystal.

He grabbed his rod, his tackle box, and the dwindling pack of smokes, not bothering to extinguish the fire. He walked back in the direction where the junkyard man had dropped him off, the pointy chunks of gravel stinging his feet. The voices screamed, and twice he doubled over as the steel bristles of a wire brush scraped and scrubbed at his insides.

On the road, he headed toward town, trying to hitchhike, but every car passed without slowing. He cursed each of them. For not stopping. For how the drivers glanced below their sun visors, took a peek, and quickly turned away as if they'd seen some horrible aberration. He cursed the world, his life, and the goddamn voices that refused to relent. "Feed us," they said. "Feed us, motherfucker."

When the bells above the door jingled, the pawnbroker smiled when he saw the familiar, haggard, drawn-out face.

"What can you give me for these?" said Henry as he placed the rod and tackle box on the counter. "Twenty? Fifteen, minimum."

The pawnbroker smiled again, already knowing he wouldn't offer more than five. And also knowing, without question, that Henry would take it.

That Time

"Bloody. That's all I'm saying. I want something bloody."

"Fine, I hear you," said Jerry, pushing away from the table. "I'll see what he's got in the garage."

Jerry was deep in his own thoughts, unaware that Doreen watched him as he headed toward the door. Unaware that she watched his thigh muscles beneath his snug, faded jeans, watched his cell phone in his front pocket rise and fall with his gait, watched how the tail of his untucked flannel wavered. He didn't see her raise a bottle of Bud and take a slug while holding a butcher knife in the other hand. He didn't notice her turn back to the counter and lop the head off a yellow onion.

His father's garage looked exactly the same as it had back when Jerry lived there nearly ten years ago. Piece of shit push mower along the wall, one of the handles bound together with a twisted coat hanger. Broken-handled shovel, broken-handled garden rake, nearly broken-handled maul, all grouped in the corner. Jerry ran his fingers along the edge of the homemade work-bench, avoiding the piles of magazines, plastic wire-nuts, rusted pliers, ancient yellowed owner's manuals ranging in scope from an Amana Radarange to the piece of shit lawnmower to the very box freezer he currently headed toward. He stepped around oil stains spread over the smooth concrete like a murder scene, sand and sawdust sprinkled about to soak up the evidence. "Jesus Christ," he mumbled, "my inheritance." He realized if Doreen had thought the attic was cluttered, well, she hadn't seen anything yet.

Was it bad that he felt bitter? That he resented having to clean out the house of all the crap his father had never bothered with, his father probably knowing all along that he'd die someday in a drunken crash, slamming his truck into a telephone pole along a road he'd traveled back from the bar thousands of times, and because of this premonition, had found that to be the perfect excuse not to tidy the place? It was just like Walker Stiles to think only of himself. Walker had often made it clear to Jerry that he thought of him not so much as a son but as a liability. When Jerry was about to graduate high school, he'd shakily brought up the idea of college with his father.

"College?" said Walker. "And you want me to pay for it? The eighteen-year full-ride I gave you wasn't enough? You want *more* school? Damn, man, I couldn't wait to finish and get the hell on with my life when I was your age."

The freezer now stood before him, waist-high, as long and boxy as a picnic table, and as Jerry approached he thought about the graduation present his father had actually given him. Not money for community college, no. Instead, a half-full bottle of Maker's Mark and a quarter ounce of dirt weed he'd grown in a drainage ditch on a neighbor's property.

So here he was now, trying to get his dead father's house in order. A few days after the funeral, the real estate agent had told Jerry to clean up the home, get it spic-and-span, because there was a prospective buyer, a Yankee, who was looking for exactly such a place. "Floyd County's cup," said the agent, "is starting to runneth over with such characters." Meaning, the buyer was one of those guys from up north with money, wanting some land and a cabin for the few times a year he might come to Virginia to shoot a deer or two. Maybe a turkey if he got real lucky.

Speaking of which, Doreen wanted some venison for a pot of chili. One thing Walker Stiles was always dependable for was a freezer chockfull of meat, mainly because he shot deer practically year round. The term "hunting season" wasn't something Walker had ever adhered to. Buck or doe, fall, winter, or spring, he didn't give a damn. He'd pulled into the driveway one June night, smiling and half-drunk as he pointed to the pickup bed for Jerry to see. Lying on a ratty blanket was a dead fawn, its neck snapped back, its white spots easily discernable.

"Just threw the headlights and stuck the nine mil out the window," he'd laughed. "Didn't even have to get out of the truck."

"You interrupted my studying for this? I've got an exam tomorrow." Jerry had turned and walked off.

"What the hell's up your ass? You all of the sudden don't eat meat? You magically..." he said, snapping his fingers, "...turned into one of those hippie vegetarians or something?"

Jerry opened the freezer lid, expecting it to be piled high with a hundred pounds of venison. Packages wrapped tightly in butcher's paper, black marker indicating what was what: hamburger, steaks, tenderloin. But there was less than twenty pounds inside. Just beneath the layer of frozen meat was a blue tarp, one Jerry immediately recognized. It had been sitting out back for what seemed like forever, covering an engine block from a Mustang that Walker had never gotten around to rebuilding. It now seemed oddly out of place. Why the hell would a tarp be taking up valuable space in the box freezer?

Jerry cleared away some of the venison until he managed to get a good hold on one end of the tarp. He wriggled it, trying to unstick it from the ice crystals lining the walls. The cold burned his hand, biting into it as he squeezed the plastic. Something was wrapped inside. Something heavy. Something he couldn't possibly lift without using both hands and, even then, he'd have to throw his back into it.

"Oh my God," a voice yelled from behind. Jerry's skin prickled as he slammed the lid. "Would you look at all this?"

"Jesus, Doreen, you scared the hell out of me."

"It's this goddamned garage you should be scared of. Look at all this shit. It'll take us a week. I think your dad was a hoarder, Jer. I swear on the Holy Bible itself, I think he might've been."

"Yeah, maybe," he said. His pulse wiggled uncomfortably in his throat.

"You find my venison or not? I mean, how long's it take? Onions and garlic are all chopped, but I need some meat."

Jerry reopened the freezer and quickly snatched a couple of packages, then banged the lid shut. "Here you go," he said, forcing a smile, trying to keep cool. He held one in each hand and playfully shook them like a set of maracas. "Dinner's on Pops."

From Jerry's perspective, his relationship with his father had been more or less normal. Whatever that meant. It was their normal anyway. Walker drank some, went down to the Pine Tavern after work most nights, but nothing crazy. He'd always fed Jerry, roof over the head, the whole nine yards. Sure he was an asshole sometimes, but what father wasn't? So he sold a little weed on the side, poached some deer, but Jerry had never thought of him as a necessarily bad man. He was gruff, yes. Blunt, yes. A bit rough around the edges, no doubt, but he wasn't evil or cruel. Had always been responsible, never missed a bill payment as far as Jerry was aware. He'd kept a steady job, the same one for over twenty-five years. Most importantly, he'd been good to Jerry's mother, had treated her like a queen mostly. Other than when she'd passed away, their lives had gone along reasonably well. Of course, there was That Time. That's the way Jerry always thought of it. That Time.

He'd been fourteen, almost fifteen, his mom dead six or seven years by then. It had been a Saturday morning when he'd heard a knock at the door. He was on the couch, eating cereal and watching *SportsCenter*, his dad still asleep after coming in much later than usual the night before.

Jerry got up, set his bowl on the table, and opened the door. Two uniformed police officers stood there.

"Hey, son," said the shorter of the two. "Your dad around?"

Jerry gulped, a partially chewed Cheerio stuck in his teeth. His face got hot, and his left foot scratched the top of his right. "He's still sleeping." He rubbed at his neck, felt moisture collecting on his fine hairs. "You want me to wake him?"

The short cop nodded. "You better go ahead and do that, son. Just tell him we got a couple questions. Nothing for you to be worried about, okay?" The cop smiled disingenuously, showed his teeth, and Jerry got nervous.

He closed the door, leaving the officers on the porch, and then wasn't sure he'd done the right thing. Should he have asked them in? Left the door ajar? He almost turned around before deciding against it. Everything in his mind felt fuzzy. For some reason he recalled his mother's final night. Those tubes in her arms. That weird cap on her head where all her hair used to be. Her cheeks so withdrawn she looked like a Buchenwald survivor. He'd seen the pictures in school. Adults who'd changed into children, children who'd transformed into adults. His mother, one of those adult-children, his mother who couldn't control her bowels and shit diarrhea on the floor or in the bed toward the very end.

As he climbed the stairs to the loft, he felt a faint embrace, almost like his mother was holding his hand, similar to that squeeze she'd given him before she fell asleep for the last time, not able to actually verbalize a goodbye.

"Pops, wake up." Jerry touched his dad's shoulder, shifted him slightly. Walker grunted. "Pops, get up."

His father suddenly sprang to attention as if pulled out of a nightmare. He looked to his right, to his left, confused. "What the hell're you doing?"

"There's two cops downstairs. They told me to wake you."

"Jesus," his father muttered, rubbing his face with the heel of his hand. And then, as if he'd just heard Jerry, "Wait, what? Cops?"

"Yeah, downstairs."

"In our house? You let them in the house?" Walker threw back the covers and scrambled out of bed, fully naked. His half-erect penis waggled back and forth, and Jerry turned away in disgust. Crumpled jeans lay on the floor, boxer shorts crammed inside. Walker grabbed the jeans, then hesitated as if remembering something. He tossed them into an overflowing hamper as he hurried around the room, his member still flopping willy-nilly.

"What the fuck, Jeremiah? Why'd you let the cops in here?"

Jerry had turned away, avoiding his father's wiry nakedness. "They're on the front porch, not in the house."

Walker pulled a clean pair of boxers from the top drawer, dancing from foot to foot as he worked them on. "What do they want? What the hell did they say?"

"I don't know." Jerry dislodged a sloggy Cheerio clump from the pit of his molar. "Just wanted to talk to you. Did you do something you shouldn't't've?"

"What? No. No, I didn't do nothing. Shit, boy, c'mon," said Walker. He had a fresh pair of jeans and a tee shirt on now. His hair was short, nearly a buzz cut, so he looked more or less presentable. Jerry saw the gears grinding in his father's head, working overtime, spinning fast, the teeth clicking, the entire network of his brain running hot. "It's probably nothing. Do me a favor," he said, nodding toward the corner, "and get a load of laundry going. Once…once I'm done talking with them, we need to get this house straight. It's been over a month without a good scrub."

"Yes, sir," said Jerry as he brushed past and went toward the hamper.

His father headed downstairs, barefooted.

In the laundry room, as Jerry loaded the clothes, he noticed the gunk on the cuffs of the wadded jeans. Mud it looked like. Mud with bits of weeds and grass packed in. Cockleburs clinging to the shins. Not exactly what you'd normally pick up at the Pine Tavern. Or on a late shift at the die casting factory.

The cops didn't take Walker down for questioning, though a few days later they did. Walker played the whole thing off, telling Jerry that apparently a pickup similar to his had been spotted in the area where that kid had gone missing. Not a kid really, a twenty-one-year-old who'd been at the tavern the same night Walker had. "Don't even remember seeing him," his dad had said. "Shit, the Pine was packed that night. Anyway, they asked me questions, just like they did to everyone. No biggie."

"Why was there mud on your jeans?" asked Jerry. It had just come out that way, without thought. Bluntly. His father started to reply then didn't bother. He simply walked off. Nothing was ever mentioned about the missing guy again.

That Time had been over ten years ago, and Jerry now recalled his boyish reasoning for never talking about it or going to the authorities. If the cops couldn't prove anything—and that was their damn job—then why should he get involved? Since they never arrested his dad, that meant he'd had nothing to do with it. But Jerry's true motive for staying silent was far more practical. He'd already lost his mother. What would happen to him if he lost his father too?

Jerry lay in bed, thinking about That Time as Doreen drunkenly rasped next to him. He'd made a point to feed her a couple extra beers. When he was sure she wouldn't wake until morning, he slipped out. A sickening roiling filled his gut. Was it possible that it was only deer shanks wrapped up in that tarp? Some larger chunks his father had never gotten around to butchering? Not likely; no hunter worth his salt would ever preserve meat that way.

Jerry had a strong suspicion he wasn't going to like what he found in that freezer.

The icy air rushed over his face, smacking him awake. Beneath the packages of meat, the blue tarp almost glowed. For an instant, when he'd first opened the lid, he'd half-expected the tarp to be gone. Even hoped it might be. But when he reached into the depths of the freezer and grasped the cold, hard plastic and felt the resistance of that very real weight, that very real heft, reality settled in.

What he knew for certain was that whatever was concealed, it most definitely *wasn't* the kid who'd gone missing ten years ago during That Time. Because that guy's body had been found a month after he disappeared, along the banks of the Little River. He hadn't drowned. Instead, he'd been strangled with something. No one had ever been charged. What investigators had never seemed to figure out, but what Jerry thought of the very same day the body was discovered was this: the far outskirts of their property, the nearly fifty mountainous acres Walker had inherited from his own daddy, that land joined the east bank of the Little River two miles or so upstream from where the body was found. From their house, it wasn't easy to get to the river, but there was a vague trail. A trail his father's riding mower and pull-behind-cart could've certainly navigated. It meandered through pine woods, then through hardwoods of oak and hickory, then a marshy bog where only skunk cabbage and jack-in-the-pulpit grew. Jerry had some-times hiked to the river to go smallmouth fishing, but once that boy's body was found, he'd never ventured there again.

The tarp crumpled and crinkled like wrapping paper. The fluorescents hummed above, one of the tubes pulsing as it strained to catch, the gas nearly spent and causing the garage to flicker in an eerie pall of purple light.

"Goddamnit," he said in a self-reprimand, "man-up and just open it already."

The loose edge of the tarp wasn't visible, so Jerry tried to roll it over as if flipping a giant blue burrito. He strained and twisted, his out of shape back muscles fight-ing in resistance, ready to rebel with spasms. But he kept heaving until he rotated the tarp within the freezer's confines. A series of grommets were spaced out in two foot intervals, the metal eyelets frosted over.

The end Jerry had been pulling on was now popping out of the freezer, resembling the tail of a fat fish too large for a cooler. He squeezed his hands into agonizing fists, then stuffed them beneath his opposite armpits, the bitter cold gnawing his fingers.

On the workbench Jerry located a pair of gardening gloves. He slipped them on, wishing—for several reasons—he'd thought of that in the first place. What was he about to get into? Did fingerprints show on frozen plastic? Oh, absolutely; he had no doubt of that. In fact, he could already see vague smudges in the frost.

He pulled the tarp edge with effort, as if unraveling a fine cigar. It didn't take long before an opening showed, and after another tug, a dark patch appeared. Jerry's insides screamed and ached. His breath increased dramatically, coming in quick, hyperventilating spurts. It was hair—shoulder length hair, pulled into a ponytail and held with an elastic Scrunchie. A woman, no question about it, her eye-shadow an indeterminate color in the poor lighting, her cheeks pale with tiny crystals prickling the skin. High cheekbones, sharp nose, bloated lips. A string of frozen blood ran from the corner of her mouth and along her cheek before disappearing behind her ear, the lobe pierced many times over with tiny silver hoops. Maybe a dozen of them. Jerry couldn't tell if she'd been pretty or not.

He pried open the tarp as far as he could until the plastic bunched at the hem of the woman's blouse. In an impulsive burst, Jerry reached inside the bundle to determine if she wore pants; that was suddenly very important to him. He only probed for a moment before the cold, brass nubs of her button-fly stung his fingertips. The fact she was clothed relieved him immeasurably. Yet at the same time, as he pulled his hand away, he was horrified. Not by the discovery of the body necessarily, though that was bothersome, but horrified because he'd become aroused. It was like part of that old Jerry—the one he'd done his damndest to suppress—was returning.

His mind flashed to two instances as a young boy. Two instances that had occasionally crept into his head over the years. Things that had made him wonder if maybe something was wrong with him. Things he never dared share with anyone, less they think him a freak. Or disturbed. Or both. Maybe the first instance was sort of normal. Just curious little boy stuff. But the other? No, something was most definitely off with that one.

In his father's trophy room were various deer heads, a red fox, several bass and trout. Also a television where Walker watched his football games. On the paneled wall was a poster of Farrah Fawcett in her bathing suit. It had always been there, even back when Jerry's mother had been alive. It was still there now. Jerry often stared at that poster as a boy, imagining removing that iconic one piece to see what was hidden beneath, to get a glimpse of that perky right nipple that teased him. One day he took a knife from the kitchen, stood on a wobbly chair, and made a slit beneath Farrah's strap. He thought if he was careful, he might be able to separate that suit from her tanned body, like skinning a rabbit, and sneak a peek at those beautiful breasts. He realized quickly that things didn't work that way, and for years he was petrified his father would notice. Jerry had been five years old.

The other instance had been in the first grade. The teacher's name was Miss Brandice. She'd been blonde, her hair always poofy, lots of makeup and very pretty. He loved her. She often wore short skirts with matching heels, usually without pantyhose, exposing her bare legs.

Jerry wanted to strap her down to a conveyor belt, much like the old movies where the damsel in distress inched ever closer to a buzz saw. But in Jerry's fantasy, there was no buzz saw, and Miss Brandice wasn't necessarily distressed. Her chest heaved and her large breasts moved on the inhale, nearly busting from her button-down blouse. Jerry wanted to rip that blouse off her. But he didn't want to hurt her. He had no thoughts of violence or harming her in any way. He just wanted to see those breasts.

For a while he'd worried about himself. Even at such a young age, he realized the thoughts and fantasies were "bad." Maybe every little boy had such thoughts, and maybe every little boy, just like Jerry, understood they shouldn't talk about them. And as time went on, those ideas faded. Mostly. As he'd matured, he'd had several serious girlfriends, and sure he'd had a dark thought here or there, but he'd always stifled them. He'd had plenty of relationships, and they'd been overwhelmingly normal. Nothing weird, nothing crazy, nothing kinky or misogynistic. He'd never gotten violent, never hurt anyone.

So why now, in the most precarious moment of his life, upon the discovery of a dead, frozen woman who his father had obviously murdered and hidden, why now, of all times in his twenty-seven years, would he get an erection? Because if there was ever a time *not* to get a hard-on, this was it. And yet his jeans were swollen at the crotch, the head of his dick dangerously close to the zipper teeth. He felt guilty. He knew it was wrong, just as he'd known as a boy that strapping his teacher to a conveyor belt was very, very bad.

"What exactly are you doing?" Doreen stumbled into the kitchen, rubbing her face, wearing nothing but an oversized tee shirt that reached her knees. She walked directly to the coffee maker and poured a cup. It was reflexive, no thought involved.

Jerry sat at the table, looking at the trees of the backyard as their silhouettes slowly came into view. Those woods where he'd played as a boy. He imagined that old fort he'd built out of pilfered 2x4s and plywood from abandoned deer stands. That fort, hidden in a copse of poplar and rhododendron, where he'd gone to sit and be alone shortly after his mother had died. *Terabithia* he'd named it, after the book. Had even taken chalk and written that word on the inside walls.

A pair of crows cawed as Jerry mumbled, "Nothing. I'm doing nothing."

Doreen, emotionless and zombie-like, opened the refrigerator, grabbed the milk, splashed her coffee. She gripped the mug with both hands, lovingly, as if holding a fragile antique. After a few sips, she seemed to become human again.

"How long you been awake, Jer? What time is it?" she said as she glanced at the microwave and answered her own question. "Not even seven yet. You okay?"

Jerry kept his eyes on the brightening backyard. "Woke up about four. Couldn't sleep."

"You want a refill or something?"

"Nah."

Doreen sat next to him, grabbed the one hand he'd left sitting limply on the table, and squeezed. "I know this is hard. It was so unexpected and all."

Jerry nodded, his chin hardly moving. "Unexpected," he said. "Yeah, that's one word for it."

"You miss your dad, don't you? I get it."

Jerry's expression was as blank as the kitchen walls. He didn't reply.

"He was a good guy. I mean, I didn't know him well, obviously, but he was sweet." She half-chuckled. "I always thought it was cute how'd he'd flirt with me."

"Jesus, shut the fuck up, Doreen. Goddamn."

She retreated quickly, pulling her hands back as if snake-bit.

For at least a minute, the only sound was the muffled caws from outside the window. Doreen kept her head down, staring at her coffee. Jerry eventually said, "I'm sorry."

Doreen whispered, "I know."

"I mean...shit. I couldn't have done all this without you. All the packing up, all the cleaning, I wouldn't've known how to even start."

"It's fine. I'm happy to help."

Jerry looked at her. "I need to talk to you, Dor." When she met his eyes, he turned back to the window, to the crows in the trees. To the pair of mourning doves sitting on the sagging clothesline. To the colors now visible, the pinks of the blooming redbuds, the whites of the dogwoods. "Need to tell you something."

"Of course. Anything."

"About my dad."

"Yeah, sure, what is it?"

He hesitated. Sitting at that table for the past few hours, he'd run through a variety of scenarios. A number of options. "I need to do the rest on my own," he said. "The packing up and all. Kind of be alone with him or whatever, you know? Be by myself for a few days, deal with all this shit."

For a beat or two, Doreen showed disappointment. Showed hurt. But she collected herself quickly. She sipped her coffee, swallowed. "Yeah, sure. I can help out this morning, this afternoon, then go to my apartment. Hell, I need to get back to work soon anyway," she said, though she'd already advised her boss she'd be out for the next few days.

"No, maybe you better get going now. Like finish your coffee and head out. And I'm sorry, Dor, I really am. I just need some alone time."

Her disappointment was more pronounced, her voice unable to hide it. She'd thought they'd be together for the long haul but now she wasn't so sure. "Okay, yeah, I'll get going here shortly."

He dropped the tarp on the cool slab of the garage floor. He'd tried to be gentle, tried to have respect, but the package was unwieldy and freezing cold, difficult to manage.

Should he lay her out, get a good look? Or just take the wrapped body, set it in the wheelbarrow as best he could, and push that thing to the deepest recesses of the property? Out near *Terabithia* most likely. Near that fort he hadn't been to in fifteen years.

He put his boots on the plastic's edge, holding it in place, and started pushing, trying to unfurl the tarp like a rolled-up carpet. Just as he'd presumed the night before, she was indeed fully clothed. Her legs looked unnatural, crooked and mangled, scrunched and bent at the knee, her open-toed sandals tucked under her rearend as if kneeling. Pieces of sharp, splintered shinbone and thighbone poked through her jeans like punji sticks. Her blouse, yellow with a paisley print, had rips along the shoulder, the skin badly scraped and scratched. What his baseball coach used to call a *strawberry* after players slid on particularly dry infields. Her shattered legs got Jerry to thinking. A car accident. His father had hit this woman with his truck. Most likely he'd been drunk. He'd panicked. It seemed plausible. And as awful as it was, Jerry felt slightly better. To him, there seemed to be a fundamental difference between covering up an accident in a moment of drunken confusion versus brutally murdering someone in cold blood.

A rectangular outline showed through the front pocket of her jeans. A pack of cigarettes maybe. Tentative at first, Jerry slid his fingers into the space. He got ahold of the object and worked it side to side. A cheap flip phone, frozen shut. When he turned it over, something was stuck to the back. He blew on it a few times, softening the crystallized grip, and pried apart a piece of paper and also a driver's license. Sarah Kramer. Date of Birth 5-14-83. Thirty years old or so. An address in Arlington, Virginia. Nearly a four-hour drive from where Jerry currently stood. The picture, though partially frosted over where somehow the cold had worked its way up and under the laminate, looked nothing like the dead girl on the garage floor. Judging by the photo, she'd been reasonably attractive. What now sat crumpled and destroyed on the tarp was anything but.

Jerry had a face, a name, an address. He had a real person versus some random body. It changed things. It made his decision harder. He set the license down and examined the paper: a ticket stub from the Interlocken Music Festival, dated September 7, 2013, nearly nine months ago. Jerry knew about it. It had taken place a couple of hours north, out in the country. Some sort of four-day Woodstock-esque hippie show. Neil Young, the remaining members of the Grateful Dead, Jimmy Cliff, and so on. Not his kind of event at all. But his father had gone. Jerry remembered stopping by the house on that Sunday, the last day of the event, to drop off the circular saw he'd borrowed, not expecting to see Walker. "What are you doing here? Thought you were still at your little sixties fest."

"Came home early. Guess I'm getting old."

Had his father seemed forlorn? Depressed? Nervous? Not that Jerry remembered. Had he ushered Jerry out of the house quicker than usual? Maybe. Walker hadn't been overly conversational but that sure as hell wasn't out of the ordinary.

Things were taking shape. The story unfolding. Walker had been partying. Drinking certainly. Maybe smoking weed. Other drugs? Jerry knew his dad's past to some degree. Walker had done his fair share. Maybe tripping on acid or rolling? Definitely possible. So he's all torn-up, gets in his truck for some reason, starts driving. This woman, Sarah, is on the side of the road, probably high herself, maybe staggers out into the lane. Walker plows into her, clips her with his bumper. Freaks out, panics, knows he's in deep shit, lifts her tiny body—hundred and twenty pounds max—and throws her into the bed of the pickup. He busts it for home, heading south on 81, making sure to go the speed limit. The three-hour drive, along with the reality of what he's done, sobers him up. He somehow makes it home safely, without incident, and finds her dead in the back. Or worse, maybe she's not dead, and Walker, in the darkest moment of his life, finishes her off. How? Jerry doesn't want to know. How he (Jerry) could have been aroused the night before mortifies him. This is real life. Real death. This woman has a family. Parents. A husband maybe. Kids possibly.

"Jesus Christ, Pops," Jerry said aloud. "What the fuck, man?"

He'd been smart about it. He didn't search for the info on his iPhone. He didn't rush to his apartment and get on his laptop. No, he'd gone to the public library. He sure as hell didn't type in Sarah Kramer or anything about her. Instead he'd searched for the Interlocken Music Festival. It didn't take long to find multiple links to the missing woman. She'd been there with two girl-friends. Had last been seen leaving the music venue alone and walking back to the camping area, a half-mile from the main stage. According to the various articles, there were no suspects, but it was an open case and had been deemed "suspicious." She was divorced, her mother still alive, a sister also, but no children. And that was the clincher for Jerry. No kids.

It had been a rainy spring. The property was soggy, but it made for easy digging. He'd wheeled her out there at night, under a starry but moonless sky. Spilled her into the hole as easily as dumping sand into a sandbox, the peepers with their incessant chirping covering up all man-made sound. Burned the driver's license, phone, and ticket stub in the woodstove the night before, on a chilly evening which had produced a frost. Nothing strange about a fire burning last night. Nothing at all. If distant neighbors had smelled wood smoke, they wouldn't have thought twice about it. Along with the body, he also buried That Time. Buried the past and all of his father's dark secrets. Also his own urges and fantasies. When he was finished, when the dead leaves and branches and twigs concealed the bare spot as naturally as if Mother Nature had done it herself, he literally, by swiping his hands back and forth to remove the dirt, wiped his hands clean of it all.

The decision hadn't been as hard as one might think. Sure, the "right" thing to do was contact the police, explain what he'd discovered, and presume everything would work out the way it was supposed to. But shit went wrong all the time. No matter what, no matter how truthful he was, there'd be suspicion cast on him. Most likely forever. Even if his entire story was absolutely, without a doubt, verified, he'd still be linked to his father. People, some people at least, would look at him differently. Would whisper this or that behind his back when he was out of earshot. *That's the guy who found the dead woman in his daddy's freezer.* And that was best case. The questioning, the media, the detectives scouring his father's house, ripping it apart, maybe discovering other things. Maybe linking his father to That Time with concrete evidence. What if there were other events Jerry didn't even know about? Other missing persons cases, perhaps. What if rumors started, saying his father had been a monster or psycho or another Jeffrey Dahmer? Jesus, did he even want to know that kind of information? And then imagine the scrutiny he'd be under. How people would treat him. He'd have to move away, but nobody would buy his father's house, or if they did, they'd get it for a song. Either he'd have to suffer for his father's doings, or Sarah Kramer's mother and sister would. And they were going to suffer either way. So the decision had been pretty simple really.

Walker had bequeathed the house to Jerry of course. Before the discovery, Jerry had been planning to sell it, make some money, move wherever he wanted. Maybe somewhere with an ocean and mango trees. The body now buried on the property changed that.

Besides the home, his father had left him a modest but surprisingly decent nest egg. He could vacate his apartment, quit his job at the shop and open up his own little garage. Maybe he'd ask Doreen to move in. Start a family, raise a few kids in the same house, on the same land, where he'd been raised. Where his father had been raised. Where Sarah Kramer was discreetly buried.

In the trophy room, Jerry pulled the tacks from the paneling and held the fragile and faded Farrah in his hands. She'd been dead for years now, cancer eating her up the same as it had his mother. But wow, Farrah had been gorgeous. That smile, that face, that hair and body. As he held the poster up to the residual sunlight streaming through the window, the slit he'd cut all those years ago was painfully obvious. With the poster lit up the way it was, almost like a photograph negative, he imagined he could see beneath her bathing suit. Could finally see the pink nipple of her rounded breast.

He poked his finger through the opening, coming at it from the back of the poster and wiggling the tip at himself as if it were a curious little worm. How could his father have never seen the cut? How had his father never confronted him about it? And then Jerry realized Walker had certainly seen it. Probably knew exactly what had happened. He imagined the scene when his father noticed it for the first time. Imagined his reaction, then the slight nod of understanding. Some things were best left undiscussed.

Jerry rolled up the poster and carefully stuffed it into the tube of an old fly rod carrier Doreen had discovered in the attic. He went to the garage and placed the tube on the top rack of a cluttered shelf. This way he'd always have access to one tiny reminder. Yes, he'd buried all of that a few nights before, but maybe he wasn't 100% ready to entirely forget his past. Maybe he was only 99.5% ready. Maybe he'd hold on to just one little keepsake, one little connection, which nobody could ever take away from him. Nobody.

Moss Man

"I never seen him directly," said Bubba, the proprietor of the Lonely Tavern, where I sat drinking a can of Pabst after my third day in town. Bubba also ran the gas station/convenience store which sold not only gas and snacks, but every plastic Jersey Devil trinket and keychain imaginable. And I'm not talking about hockey team souvenirs. I'm talking about various replicas of the beast who had supposedly haunted the area for the last two centuries. Distorted face, elongated fangs, little T-Rex arms with bent wrists, veiny batwings protruding from its back. That's the Jersey Devil I mean.

Bubba didn't look like he should've been named Bubba at all. Tall and thin with white hair, sixty-ish, and a pair of over-sized glasses, he looked more like a Kenneth or Stuart. He stood behind the lacquered bar, sipping on a draft while I sat on a stool next to Katherine, the owner of the adjoining Lonely Tavern Lodge where I'd been residing. The pair had become my acquaintances each evening after I'd been out talking to people, driving around the desolate swamps and bogs trying to gather info from the locals (or Pineys, as they preferred) who, more often than not, weren't overly excited to speak with me.

"The whole thing's bullshit," said Katherine, whose rough voice could be attributed—at least in part—to cigarettes, one of which currently wobbled between her lips. Apparently, Chris Christie's state-wide smoking ban in restaurants and bars didn't apply here. A hard woman, this one was. I'd smelled liquor on her breath that first morning when I'd strolled into the lobby to get a room. "But bullshit or not," she said, "the Jersey Devil's the only reason me and Bubba can scratch two dimes together, so I'm thankful to have him around. Tourists eat it up."

She finished her beer, and Bubba grabbed the empty glass without being asked. He angled it beneath the tap, expertly drawing a head that bulged over the rim like a white, foamy muffin-top. That exact ritual had probably been repeated tens of thousands of times. Hell, I'd witnessed nearly a dozen refills within the past two hours, with no money exchanged. Yet Katherine was as steady and even-keeled as the sturdiest ship.

"You've probably heard fifteen variations already," said Bubba. "Everybody's got their own version, but I've lived here all my life and my story's been passed down all the way back from my great-great-granddaddy."

"Okay, I'll bite," I said. I opened my pad and flipped through the notes for my article. My boss had sent me south to the sweltering, bug-infested Pine Barrens to inquire about the mutilated carcasses that had been showing up lately. Possum, deer, even a bobcat, their bones snapped and twisted, their pelts peeled back from their bodies. It was impossible not to discuss the Devil when such things occurred, and if I could spin it, I would. As my boss had told me, "The Jersey Devil sells copy. Period."

I lifted my empty, gave it a little shake in Bubba's direction. He pulled a fresh one from the cooler. I clicked my pen, dated a clean page. "Go ahead, lay it on me."

"Well, in the late 1700s," said Bubba, "a woman named Mrs. Leeds birthed her thirteenth baby. But it wasn't normal. Instead, it was some sort of hideous monster. A winged creature with hooves and a tail. Some say the head of a goat. The doctor, he bolts, not even bothering to cut the cord. Mr. Leeds, he follows the doctor right out the door. Not to bring him back, mind you, but to run off and hang himself from the closest tree.

"Mrs. Leeds, left to her own devices, rummages through the doctor's bag, finds scissors, and snips the cord herself. The thing—her own offspring—is hissing and spitting, angry and mean, but Mrs. Leeds was angrier and meaner. She picked it up at the base of its tail, holding it upside down like a caught chicken, and tromps a half mile to Miller's Bog. She drops the thing in the muck, leaving it there to drown. But of course it didn't drown, and it's been flying around ever since, feasting mainly on animals, but the occasional person goes missing too."

I sipped on my Pabst, amused with Bubba's earnestness. "And you've never seen him?"

"Not straight away. Though on two occasions, right at dusk, I've glimpsed a strange shadow scoot over me. Kind of like the way you every-once-in-awhile see a hawk's shadow, you know, gliding over the ground? And each encounter shot a chill up my back. Left me feeling cold. On that second occasion, that very same night after I'd seen it," he said, looking directly at Katherine as if her nod of affirmation would give the story validity, "that Simpson girl went missing. Snatched right out of her house. Never found her. You remember that?"

Katherine extinguished her cigarette into a plastic Budweiser ashtray, immediately lit another. "Yeah, I remember, but no goddamned devil stole her. That girl was sixteen, had met a blackjack dealer in AC. Ran off after that fella got her a fake ID. They say she's been working in one of Trump's casinos ever since."

Bubba's face reddened. "More people around here believe in it than not." He glanced at me as he pushed his glasses up the bridge of his nose. "Old Katherine's just grown bitter."

Katherine exhaled, letting some of the smoke snake back through her nose in a French inhale. "You really want a good story," she said, "then you ought find the Moss Man. Now that's a fella to write about."

Bubba immediately shook his head, scowling at Katherine.

But it was too late; my ears were perked. "Moss Man?"

"Don't go bothering Bill," muttered Bubba. "He's an old Piney who don't like to be disturbed. Lives way out in the thick of the Barrens."

My scalp tingled—journalist instinct. I had to talk with him, no doubt about it.

"Tell me more," I said, looking directly at Katherine. Then to Bubba, "And put her drinks on my tab."

Bubba rubbed the bar-top with a rag, pushing circles into the wood though there was nothing to clean. Through clenched teeth, he grumbled something inaudible. And then, much clearer, "Whatever you do, don't bring up his family."

I didn't squeeze much more out of Katherine, as Bubba grew increasingly irritated and eventually cut her off. But I did learn that the Moss Man lived alone, making money by gathering what the Pine Barrens offered. I also got a rough set of directions. Emphasis on *rough*. Things like "Turn at the bridge, go five miles to green dumpster. Make a left by a giant sycamore."

Using Katherine's final marker—a rusted "No Hunting" sign nailed to a tree at a sharp bend—I veered onto a lane that was hardly wide enough for my little Jetta to fit through. Moss Man's driveway: two bare patches, knee-high weeds Mohawking the middle. My car jostled over the bumps and runnels, and I felt sure the guts of my transmission would rip out. The morning was hot, and with my window down, chirping frogs superseded everything. There must've been millions of them, singing eerie springtime love songs. In a different setting, it might have been pleasant and peaceful.

At the lane's end, dense trees gave way to a clearing. An old shack with warped boards faded to gray sat in the opening. A stone chimney, somewhat askew, poked from a tin roof muddied to rusty orange. Despite the heat, a trace of smoke trickled out. A 1960s pickup—tailgate gone, fender dented, pocks of rust on the passenger door—sat in front.

I parked behind the truck, the chirrup of frogs even more intense after killing the engine. The yard, or what I'm calling a yard, consisted of low-lying weeds clinging to a soft, sandy soil. Parallel lines were scratched into the dirt, and it took a second to realize the entire grounds had recently been raked.

"Bill?" I called with unease. A quiet had overtaken the place. As soon as I yelled, every little frog shut the hell up as if I'd rudely broken etiquette. I beckoned again, waiting for a vicious dog to bust from the barn, but got no reply, not even from the frogs.

Three swaybacked steps led to the front porch, which housed a rocking chair. Then I noticed the flowers. Not standard geraniums or pansies. I'm talking exotic flowers. Whites, pinks, purples—blooms popping out all over. They were part of the house, clinging and growing straight from the porch railings instead of in pots, some of the root systems wrapping around the support posts like snakes encircling a staff.

Because of the flowers, the place had a charming, Hansel-and-Gretel-ish feel, which, after contemplating that comparison for a moment, I wasn't overly comfortable with. I was literally in the middle of nowhere. In the Jersey Devil's stomping grounds, which, up until then, was a notion I'd only found amusing. The way Bubba and the other Pineys believed in him so devoutly was what I would've attributed to—only a few days before—ignorance, naiveté, or blind faith. But now I wasn't so sure. The isolation, the forest's darkness, the silence, it all gave a bit more credence to believing some infamous creature lurked in the swamps.

The porch-boards sighed as I climbed. The two windows bookending the door were blocked by a combination of shades and thick curtains. As I went to knock, someone spoke. I wheeled around to find a man at the bottom of the steps, eyeing me in a not-so-friendly manner.

"Bill?"

"I'm Bill," said the man, "but that's not what I asked. I said, 'Who're *you*?' And what's the whys of you trespassing?"

He was thin, his long-sleeved flannel and jeans so loose they looked borrowed. His beard, thick and a silvery gray, matched the house's facing boards. Katherine had said he was mid-seventies, and upon first glance, that seemed right. But when I looked deeper he had one of those faces, hidden beneath his beard, that could've been plus-or-minus fifteen years of seventy. Part of that agelessness was his eyes. They were a piercing blue, nearly robin's egg, which I'd never seen before. Maybe on a Siberian Husky, but not on a man.

"My name's Dave Hamilton," I said, nervously extending my hand. "How're you? I'm with the *Star-Ledger*. Up in Newark. Would it be okay if I asked you a couple of questions?"

Bill licked his lips. "To question one, I'm fine. And to question two, it would be okay except you've already done it."

I tilted my head. "I'm sorry?"

"*Can you ask me a* couple *of questions.* You already did, and I've answered them. So are we done? Can I go ahead and shoot you now?"

My mouth opened but nothing came out. He moved a hand behind him, letting it rest near the small of his back. "I'm only messing with you, pal," he said, letting out a deep laugh. "Don't get a lot of visitors. Which is the way I like it. But you caught me on a good day. What do you want to know?"

I forced a laugh, then retracted my hand since he didn't seem interested in shaking it. "I'm doing a story on the Jersey Devil. There's been reports of mutilated animals. Somebody suggested I talk to you."

"Um-hmm. And who's this somebody?"

"Katherine? From the Lonely Tavern?"

Bill nodded. "That's a woman who'll make you curse the son-of-a-bitch who invented liquor. Got a bite like a copperhead."

I laughed again, this time more naturally. "She does seem to know how to toss them back."

"Good enough girl though, at least when she was young. And tough as a pine knot. Same as her daddy."

"Yeah, that's what I gathered. Anyway, she said you might have a theory about those animals. And maybe the Jersey Devil."

"I got work to do, but if you want to come along, I don't mind jawing. But those dead animals? That's the work of coyotes," he said, pronouncing it *ki-oats*. "Not any devil. Been seeing them more and more lately. They're mean, tough little SOBs." He pulled a sleeve of sunflower seeds from his pocket and poured a few into his mouth. "They'd give Katherine a good run for her money, that's for damn sure."

I flipped open my pad and scratched some notes. Bill worked the seeds like a plug of chaw, spitting out the shells.

"Is that all you got to wear?" he said, eyeing my Timberlands.

"My boots? Yeah, that's all I've got. Why?"

He shook his head, spit a few more shells. "Those things wouldn't last ten minutes where we're going."

I examined my boots, less than a week old. "What do you mean? I paid over a hundred bucks for these things. Bought them just for this trip."

"Come on," he said as he walked off.

In the barn's dark shadows, he removed a pair of hip waders hanging from a sixteen penny nail. "Take off your hundred dollar boots and put on these rubbers. Got 'em for ten dollars back in 1975. Impressed?" He didn't look at me with derision exactly; it was more like bemusement. Before I could answer, he pointed toward a hay bale. "Sit down there, slide 'em on, and we'll go. I'll get the barrow."

I took a seat, but to my surprise the hay bale wasn't a hay bale at all. I sank several inches, and when I used my hands to brace myself, the material was soft and spongy. As my eyes adjusted to the dark, vague images of rectangular moss bales appeared, each secured with twine. There must have been a hundred of them, the aroma rich and earthy.

I exchanged my Timberlands for the waders. Behind me, a wheel squeak was followed by Bill saying, "You ready?"

"Sure. We going to collect moss?"

The night before, Katherine had informed me that Bill made his living by selling sphagnum moss to local nurseries and flower shops. And I'd been fascinated by that.

Bill took another shot of sunflower seeds. "Boy, they sure grow 'em sharp up there at the *Star-Ledger*, don't they?"

I reddened, feeling a bit foolish.

"I'm just busting your chops, there, pal. You want a story about the Jersey Devil, well, thought I'd show you where he lives. Might as well get a little work done while I'm at it, right? You're working, I'm working."

Bill stepped out of the barn shadow, pushing the wheelbarrow into the morning light. It was the biggest one I'd ever seen, twice as deep as any the Home Depot carried.

"That seems like a good tool to bring along," I said, trying to joke, motioning toward the pitchfork resting in the wheelbarrow's cavity. "Kind of apropos considering we're going devil hunting."

The old man didn't laugh or even smile. "Use it to loosen the moss."

I sidled up, my pad and pencil at the ready. "Before we start, can I get your full name?" I said, scratching the date into the upper right corner.

He spat a glob of shells. "You best put away your little book and pencil. I never yet seen a man who could push a barrow with one hand. Damn near impossible."

He started toward the forest where several faint trails wiggled through the trees in different directions. I pocketed my pad, grabbed the handles, and hefted the giant wheelbarrow before hustling after him. But he'd already vanished. As quietly as fog dissipating over a river.

The sunshine dimmed once we got into the thick of it. I followed, navigating the wheelbarrow along the narrow path, the pitchfork tines clanging against the worn metal tub. Bill didn't look back or bother talking, and I had to give it to him, the old guy could motor. He hopped over downed trees like a deer, bobbed and weaved through low branches like a graceful boxer.

The deeper we went, the more anxious I became. The

tall pines stood in formation, sentry-like, the forest floor a carpet of dead needles and creeping moss. And it was so quiet. As Bill trudged on, I noticed a squelch beneath my feet. With every step, it got worse, the wheelbarrow harder to push as the tire slurped in the bogginess. I immediately appreciated the waders.

A mile in, Bill stopped, waiting for me. As I schlepped toward him, an annoying whine rang in my ears. Then a mosquito drilled my arm, followed by several more. Bill seemed amused when I tried to smack them. He pulled a handful of moss from the ground. "Rub this on you."

I slapped at my forearm again. "You got any bug spray? Some OFF or something?"

"Yeah, I sure do," he said. "Right here next to my hairspray and tampons. Just give me a minute to rummage through my purse."

I smacked again. "You're a real funny guy, Bill. Let me tell you, a real funny guy."

"Take the goddamned moss already."

I grabbed the clump and rubbed it over my exposed areas. It smelled like dirt but, I have to admit, immediately did the trick.

Bill winked. "You can leave that stuff here," he said, indicating the wheelbarrow and pitchfork. "We're going off-road for a few."

The ground became even soupier. Like slogging through fresh concrete. Yet Bill moved deftly, slicing through briar thickets and copses of trees. At one point I stepped on a plant that emitted an awful odor.

"Skunk cabbage," he said. "You ought to avoid that."

"You might've warned me beforehand," I said, plugging my nose.

"A jackass learns to plow a row by doing, not by being told."

We reached the edge of a murky pond, the water stagnant and black. The sky had gone overcast, a soaring red-tailed hawk offering the only contrast. The water was so dark that the mirrored bird zipped across the surface, only dissipating when the image collided with the tops of a few snapped trees poking through the water, their branches gnarled and twisted. I imagined strange tree-people lurking below, trying to fight their way to the top. The eeriness had returned, and if Bill had decided to run off right then, I'd have been screwed. Even in the thick humidity, a chill ran up my arms.

"So what's this place?"

Bill looked out over the pond, two hundred yards across and surrounded by the green heads of pines. He seemed to be in deep reflection. "His home," he said.

"*His home?* What do you mean? Whose home?"

Bill didn't reply.

"You mean the Jersey Devil lives near this pond?"

"In it."

"In it? How does he live *in it?* I thought he was some sort of flying winged creature."

"He might have wings, can't say for sure, but this is

where he lives…far as I'm concerned."

"You've seen him here before? In this pond?" With the others I'd interviewed, the mood had been light, mainly because I thought the whole thing was a lark. Some urban legend people took a little too seriously. But with Bill it was different. He was so damn grave all of the sudden.

"It's been nearly fifty years…" he said, soft and monotone, "…but this is the place."

I forced a faint chuckle, attempting to put myself at ease. "Care to expound?"

"Care to *what?*"

"Expound. Explain. As in, tell me what happened?"

Bill cupped his bearded chin, eyeing the dark, placid water as if trying to see beneath the surface. As if searching for something he'd lost. "Nope." He then headed back into the forest. The hawk had vanished.

I fumbled with my iPhone and snapped some pictures. Then I jogged to catch up, asking myself what in the hell I was doing out there.

Back at the wheelbarrow, Bill had shut off. I asked a few questions but he wouldn't say a word. Instead, he shoved that fork into the ground, pulling up moss, meticulously working his fingers through it, dropping some into the wheelbarrow while discarding other pieces. It all looked the same to me, grayish-brown blobs, but he saw things I didn't.

Once full, I pushed the load. Along the way, I'd seen more of those same exotic flowers clinging to various tree trunks. I asked about them as we neared the barn, and finally Bill answered. It was as if being back on his own land snapped him out of his funk.

"Those aren't just flowers," he said. "They're orchids."

"Same as the ones on your porch, right?"

"Yep. They say money don't grow on trees, but I beg to differ."

"How's that?" I said, relieved to have him talking again.

"Besides all the moss, the nurseries buy up the orchids I collect. There's money to be made just about anywhere, long as you know where to look."

I dumped the moss in a corner of the barn. I anticipated being sore in the morning. My arms were fatigued, my calves taut. Scratches crossed my hands while mosquito welts bubbled my neck and forearms. Yet Bill appeared unscathed. I removed the waders and laced my boots.

I met him on the porch where he casually rocked, assuming we'd go inside to wash up, but he made no such offering. "Well, thanks for your help," he said instead, chewing on sunflower seeds. "I've pushed that barrow upwards of ten thousand times I'd say. Nice to have a morning off."

"No problem," I said, probing the muscles near my elbow. "You think I could use your bathroom? Maybe wash my hands and take a leak before I head back?"

"Nope. I'd rather you not." He shifted in his chair.

The tightly drawn shades covering the two front windows made me want to see inside that house. Badly. I wanted to understand how he lived. "Come on, Bill. I've really got to go. Need to rinse this mud off, too."

Bill started rocking again. "There's a wash bucket around the corner if you need it. And the world's your bathroom. Can't take a piss in your own yard then your yard ain't worth a piss."

He wasn't going to budge, and for some reason, a part of me started to believe maybe there was some truth to this Jersey Devil stuff. It went against all my innate logic and reason, but whatever secrets he was holding onto, I had no doubt they were in that house.

"Listen, you mind if I come back tomorrow?"

"You don't want to be here tomorrow. There's a gulley-washer coming."

There wasn't one cloud in the sky, which struck me as odd because back at the pond things had been overcast. I was sure of it. I'd also watched the forecast on the local news that morning. "They're not calling for rain anytime in the next five days."

"I don't know who *they* is," said Bill, "but *they* is wrong. It's gonna be a frog choker."

"The weatherman said otherwise."

"Weatherman?" scoffed Bill. "You don't need a weatherman to know which way the wind blows."

I laughed. "If I use that in my article, should I quote you or Dylan?"

Bill looked at me blankly, his eyes saying he'd never met a bigger fool. "Me or *who*?"

"Never mind. Forget it," I said. "Would it be all right if I come by again, next time the weather's nice?"

Bill spat a mishmash of shells over the railing. "I suppose that'd be fine. Don't know what good it'll do, but I'll be here."

When I got back to the lodge a half-hour later, a distant boom of thunder rolled across the sky, a stack of cauliflower clouds building on the horizon.

A day-and-a-half after Bill's correctly predicted deluge, I approached his porch again. But this time I came with a different attitude, mainly because of what I'd learned from Katherine and Bubba. We'd had a few drinks when Katherine opened up about some unimaginable things concerning Bill. It was horrific, and as much as I didn't want to ask him about it, the journalist in me said I had to.

He sat in the rocking chair when I arrived, my waders bunched at his feet as if expecting me. The orchids around the columns had turned their little faces to the early sunshine. "Morning, Bill. How you doing today?"

"Fair to midlin'," he said, sipping coffee.

"It's a pretty morning. Was wondering if we might talk?"

"That'd be fine, but I got work to do."

"Don't suppose you've got an extra cup?" I said, wanting more than anything to get a look inside that house, to perhaps dispel the rumors I'd heard.

Bill hoisted himself slowly out of the chair. His body, despite easily outworking mine the other day, was thin and frail. His back was permanently hunched, albeit slightly, as if leaning into a stiff wind. The veins on his hands poked through like green worms; his throat dewlaps drooped loosely. Whatever mirage I'd seen that first day had vanished. Bill no longer seemed ageless. Now, he just looked old.

He turned the doorknob, with me right behind. But before he even cracked it, he said, "Cream and sugar? Or black?"

"I can pour it myself. Just tell me where you keep the cups."

"You put on your rubbers," he said, careful not to push the door open. "I'll be back in a minute."

"I really don't mind getting it."

"Cream and sugar? Or black?"

"Black."

"Good, cause I don't have any cream and sugar." That spark in his eyes had returned.

The rest of the day found Bill in excellent humor. His disposition hadn't shifted or changed the way it had after he'd shown me the pond. It wasn't until we were finished, after I'd pushed three wheelbarrow loads, that I decided to mention his family. Except I was nervous and found any excuse to avoid the topic.

"Those orchids are beautiful," I said as I removed the waders. "You think maybe tomorrow we could go out and find one for me to take home? I'm heading back north in the afternoon."

"I can just pot you up one of these right quick. No charge. I got milk cartons I use."

I saw the milk cartons as my chance to finally get in

the house. When I'd mentioned to Katherine and Bubba about how Bill hadn't wanted me inside that day, they'd both nodded. Katherine had said, "One time a nursery guy sliced his hand wide open on his tailgate while loading Bill's moss bales. Bleeding bad. He wanted to run water over it in the kitchen, but Bill found a rag, wrapped the man's hand, then sent him on his way."

"Yeah, he was the same way with me," I'd said.

Katherine had paused to blow a stream of smoke upward. "Some say he's captured the Devil. Has him chained up in the cellar. Don't necessarily believe it myself, but that's what some swear by."

"Sure, I'd love a potted plant," I said. "If you don't mind."

"Cartons are in the barn, against the back wall. Go grab one and pick out whichever orchid you want."

I hesitated. "On second thought, I want to choose my very own. From the wild."

"Ah, I get it. Got yourself a lady back home?"

"Well, not so much anymore." I hesitated again. "I'm in the middle of a divorce, actually."

Bill nodded. "Relationships can be tricky."

And just like that, without even trying, what I'd wanted to ask was right there in front of me. "You ever been married, Bill?"

"Never did have much luck with marriage," he said. "Married three different times."

Now here it was. I didn't know there'd been *three* wives. Katherine had only mentioned the one, and a couple of kids, too. "So you're familiar with divorce too, huh?"

"Nope, not divorce. My first wife, when I was still quite young, she was murdered."

"What?"

"Yep. They never caught the guy. And my second wife, a few years later, well, she died from eating poisonous mushrooms."

"Man, I don't know what to say."

Bill rocked in his chair, solemnly. "That's all right. Not much you *can* say. And my third wife, well, she died from being beaten over the head with a baseball bat."

"Goddamn, Bill. I'm..." But I didn't finish. An apology would've been pointless.

Bill nodded as he stopped rocking. "Yeah, the last one, with the baseball bat, that happened because the stubborn old thing refused to eat the poisonous mushrooms." And then he let out a cackle that echoed off the surrounding pine trunks. I paused before joining him.

When we finally calmed, he said, "I'll see you tomorrow, there, pal."

Going to the lodge, I reflected on what Katherine had told me the night before. About what had really happened to Bill's wife, understanding why he'd been so pensive while showing me the pond that day.

"Happened in the early-sixties," Katherine had said. "I was in second grade. We'd had a rough winter. Most people lost power for weeks because of an ice storm. But word still got around. And I knew it was true for sure when I went to school, because Bill's little girl, Sophie, didn't show up. Teacher informed our class, but I refused to buy it. It took another month of seeing Sophie's empty desk before I finally wrapped my head around it. If there'd been a funeral, then maybe I'd have believed sooner. But you couldn't have a funeral without a body.

"From all accounts, Bill was a good husband to Caroline. Good father, too. Sophie was eight and her little brother, whose name I don't even remember, was six."

"Lawrence," said Bubba, drinking from his glass of draft. "His name was Lawrence."

"Right, Lawrence," said Katherine. "Bill had taken the kids and Caroline ice skating, some pond in the middle of the Barrens. They'd been skating when Sophie strayed toward an area where a moving creek filtered in. Caroline went after Sophie, pulling Lawrence along, while Bill was out in the middle, making figure eights or some such. Next thing Bill knows, there's a horrible *pop*, some screams, and by the time he gets halfway to them, all three have gone under. Swallowed up. Sucked down. My daddy told me Bill plunged right into that hole. Dove head-first, but they were gone. Said Bill nearly died too, and, I imagine, probably would've preferred if he had. Ever since, he's lived out at that place all alone, never quite the same. And who could blame him? Just crawled up inside himself and shut the world out."

"Damn," I said.

"Yeah, damn. Of course there's other theories out there, too."

"Such as?"

"You do the math," said Katherine. "No bodies ever recovered. Bill turning all sorts of secretive. Not too hard to figure that rumors would get started. But the cops never pursued it, far as I know."

That final morning, as I walked toward Bill's porch, he sat in his rocking chair as usual. As I mounted the three steps, I said, "Hey, old man, how's it going?"

He didn't reply, and it took a second to realize he was napping. I spoke again, louder, and then I knew. I nudged the curved bottom rail of the rocking chair with my Timberland, moving it forward and back.

"Goddamnit, Bill," I said. I didn't want to touch him. I'd held a dead dog once when I was a boy, after it got run over by my neighbor, and it messed with my head for months.

I had never checked a pulse, nor did I have any idea how to actually do it, but when I grabbed Bill's wrist, his skin was cold. Or not cold exactly, but certainly not warm like it was supposed to be. His eyes were closed, his mouth slightly ajar as if whistling.

I reached for my phone, ready to call 9-1-1 when I noticed something, partially hidden by the chair. It was an orchid, standing about knee-high, and potted in a plastic milk carton cut in half, the base packed tightly with fresh moss. The flowers were open, white with flecks of purple spotting the petals. I stared at the orchid, then at the closed front door. And that's when I put the phone back in my pocket. After all, at this point, what was the rush?

Was I expecting to find some chained beast inside, foaming at the mouth and utterly hideous? Some vicious winged creature whose mother had attempted to murder it? Or maybe Bill's own family, old now, imprisoned for fifty years? Of course not. But I'd be lying if I said I hadn't thought about such things.

The door opened to the living room: a couple of floral-patterned upholstered chairs, a crocheted granny-squared afghan draped over a loveseat, an enormous console television. But I was immediately drawn to a bookshelf filled not with books but record albums. In front of the bookshelf was a phonograph with one stray album cover sitting next to it, noticeable because it was the only thing out of place. A young Bob Dylan stared back at me. I picked it up, fanning myself, and chuckled, "You sly son of a bitch."

The kitchen was as neat and orderly as the living room: white refrigerator that reminded me of my grandmother's, shaped like a rounded bullet. Breadbox and toaster on the counter. Pots and pans hanging from hooks above a woodstove. But the kitchen table was what caused my stomach to drop, what prickled my skin as if racked with fever.

A pair of children sat at the table, a girl and a smaller boy, empty plates in front of them. And behind the children, a woman stood dressed only in an apron, hunched over as if about to pick up one of the plates. But they weren't real, living people. Instead they were replicas, frozen in time, completely fashioned out of dried moss. The woman had an hourglass shape to her, even faint humps for breasts. Though the face had no distinct features per se, somehow she was almost attracttive. Maybe it was the prominent cheekbones, or perhaps the shoulder-length blonde hair, made from what appeared to be bleached moss. At each end of the table were unoccupied chairs though each spot had a complete place setting, as if the entire family was about to sit down to breakfast.

An immediate thought came to mind. Of those people in Nagasaki who'd been obliterated by the bomb, their white silhouettes smeared on blackened walls as they'd walked down the street. Their shadows the only reminders of lives completely evaporated.

There was an eeriness to that image which I now equated to the moss family, yet it was touching and beautiful, too. A family frozen in time.

I wanted to touch them but somehow it felt wrong. Felt like a direct violation of Bill and his privacy. I decided it was time to call 9-1-1 but then hesitated. What would Bill want me to do? Would he want the whole community to know he'd kept a moss family in his house as some sort of homage? Did I want people going around talking about Bill as if he was a deranged, troubled freak? Because I knew damn well people would create all sorts of stories, make up rumors—just as they had before—many of them depraved and perverted. Bill deserved better.

So one-by-one, I picked up the family and carried each out the front door, where Bill watched silently from his rocking chair. I paused momentarily with each passing to let him say his final goodbyes, and then I took first little Sophie, then Lawrence, and finally Caroline to the edge of the woods, where I carefully dismantled them, unknotting the twine that held their bodies together, as well as the underlying pine limbs that had acted as the framework. Stick figures, in the most literal sense. I kept looking over my shoulder as I worked. What if somebody caught me? What if somebody witnessed me tearing the family apart? What would they do? What would *I* do?

I dispersed the moss and limbs into the woods, destroying the evidence. No one in a million years would be any the wiser to the love and compassion Bill had had for his family. No one would know how badly he had missed them. And I believe that's the way he wanted it.

Back at the house, I washed my hands in the sink, dried off, then walked down the hall, compelled to see the rest of the home. There were two bedrooms, the back one obviously Bill's, while the other had two small single beds, one with a pink bedspread, the other red. A stuffed bear and a Raggedy Ann lay on the pink bed, and in the corner of the room were several toys. A yellow metal Tonka trunk, a hula-hoop, a miniature Radio Flyer.

As I was about to exit, the faintest little something on Lawrence's bed caught my eye. It was tightly made, the bedspread folded back just beneath the single pillow. And it was there that I now focused. Two or three strands of moss, barely noticeable, stood out in contrast to the white pillowcase. Like fine hairs left by someone who'd been sleeping.

I stepped over to Sophie's bed, where I observed something similar. A few more wisps on the pink covers. I didn't bother to check Bill's bed but imagined the same on Caroline's side. And probably, if I'd examined the living room, I might've found more moss on the chairs and loveseat, where the family perhaps once gathered to watch *Bonanza* or *The Dick Van Dyke Show* but were now stuck with *American Idol* or, God forbid, *Jersey Shore*. Those little strands of moss scattered about were like fibers at a crime scene, painting the full picture of Bill's lonely existence.

I stepped outside, grabbed the milk carton, and sat on the top stair. I angled my body so I was more-or-less facing Bill. Between thumb and finger, as if examining expensive fabric, I gently caressed the petals of the orchid. Then I pulled out my phone and dialed.

My heart pounded when the other end started ringing. Bill's corpse watched me intently, as if listening. Or at least hoping I was smart enough to say the right thing.

Jim Limey's Confession

As told to his granddaughter, Rita Limey Phillips, on October 19th, 1993, several days before his death in Weems, Virginia.

My daddy's name, your great granddaddy, was Robert Limey. At least that's what the white folks started calling him after he went into business for his own self, back when I was just a baby. I guess he didn't ever see no reason to correct them. When he got killed, about 1922, I think it was, I took over the business. I was somewhere around thirteen, fourteen years old, and not at all ready for my daddy to be gone.

The day after Daddy went in the ground, it was time for me to get to work. I was the man of the family then, and it was up to me to take over the business. I'd been going around with Daddy some anyway, so I knew most everything there was to know about it. I hitched Miss Annabelle to the wagon, loaded up the barrels of lime, then headed to town.

We made all the lime right there on the property. Daddy'd been a smart man and figured it all out his own self. He built a stone kiln and used shells from all along the riverbanks of the Rappahannock. He used to pay us boys a penny a sackful. There were shoals along the river where it was nothing but crushed shells. Whole bars you could walk on that reached way out into the water— shoot, nearly all the way to the Chesapeake Bay itself. Clam shells and oyster shells, all bleached white from sitting in the sunshine for a hundred years. Daddy worked four days a week making lime in the kiln, and the other two on privy duty. Sunday was church and rest. So that's where I was headed with Miss Annabelle that first day after Daddy'd been buried, going to town for privy duty.

There were about fifty privies spread throughout Weems that we took care of, most in town, some out in the country. Lots of farmers used the lime for their corn and peanut crops, too, so that's why Daddy spent so much time making it, because everyone needed it for something or other. You can make a fair dime in lime, that's what he always said.

There wasn't much to it really, privy duty. I had me a steel shovel that I'd scoop the stuff out with. At the back of each privy was a plank, blocking the opening. I'd slide out the plank and then shovel the slop, dumping it into a slatted whiskey barrel sitting on the wagon. At the end of the day, I'd empty the barrel in the woods down at the far end of our property. You've never seen so many flies in all your life as when you're pouring human muck into a privy pit. You've also never seen a place so bright green come springtime.

After I emptied a privy, then I'd go inside and lime the hole. Every privy had a small little bucket on the floor which I kept filled so they could do it themselves if it got to smelling real sharp. In the winter it wasn't too bad. Summertime was the worst; that's when things got ripe. It could knock out a dead man when that stink got all mixed up with the heat and humidity. Almost taste it sometimes. I'd use me a hanky to cover up with if it was really powerful, but only when I knew nobody was home. White folks didn't like to see a Negro covering up his face at the smell of their business.

I charged a nickel a week. If no one was home to pay me, I'd just leave a tiny heap of lime, no more than a handful, down on the floor at the base of the commode. That way they'd know that I come by, and I'd just collect the following week. Daddy kept track of it all in his head, and I did the same. Of course, just after he died, I didn't know who owed what, but most folks were real good about it and paid what was due.

There was one man, though, who was just plain hateful. Crooked as a barrel full of fish hooks. Wendell Burroughs. Never had a kind word for nobody. He was short and beanpole skinny, but you could tell he was strong. When he did something as simple as grab a shovel handle, his muscles rippled like pond water. His face and arms were burnt red from making his living off the land, had hair that looked like a mercury-shined nickel. He lived in a tiny shotgun house on the far end of Dr. Love's property, tucked way back in the woods and off to itself.

The first day I showed up without Daddy, he was on the front porch atop a steep set of rickety stairs, glaring with hateful eyes down across the yard. The privy was seventy-five feet from the steps, and I'd gone straight to work, not wanting at all to mess with him. I'd seen how he talked to Daddy before, and I didn't expect he'd be no nicer to me.

"Heard your daddy's dead, boy," he called from the porch as I dumped the first shovelful of slop into the whiskey barrel.

"Yes, sir," I said. "Passed Saturday evening."

"Well, I didn't owe him nothing, and I don't got no money for you, neither," he said. "Not today anyways." As he climbed down the steps and into the yard, he gimped along like an old mutt with a bad paw.

"That's all right, Mr. Burroughs. You can pay next week." I went around to the back of the privy for another shovelful.

"Goddamn, boy, you'd probably go around your elbow to get to your thumb, seeing as how you're doing it. Your daddy done it lickety-split."

I'd learned early on to just zip my mouth shut and keep working when dealing with white folks like Wendell Burroughs. I finished up and scatted out of there fast, repeating to him that next week would be just fine for payment.

Now, Dr. Love couldn't have been more different than Wendell Burroughs. A fine man and always kindly to me. Had a fancy house on the west corner of the square in Weems, with long white columns out on the front porch that stretched all the way to the roof. Thick oaks and sycamores shaded the yard, and pretty crepe myrtles added bursts of red all around the property. He loved those crepe myrtles, and lots of times he'd be out in the yard trimming and shaping them. Loved them so much that he named his daughter Myrtle May Love. She was born shortly after Daddy died, and over the years that little girl grew on me.

Myrtle May was about the sweetest thing you ever did see. Looked just like that Shirley Temple that was in the movies a few years later. She wore the same frilly dresses, had fluffy locks hanging from her head like little blonde sausages. Big blue eyes, too. She was the cutest thing, and you could tell she was everything to Dr. Love. He was getting on in years and had never had any children until Myrtle May come along.

She'd always follow me around the yard when I come by. Often times, she'd have a baby-doll in one hand and a carrot in the other.

"Hey, Jim Limey," she'd say, "you reckon I can feed your horsey a carrot."

Now Miss Annabelle was a mule, not a horse, but it didn't make no difference to me, I just told her to go right ahead. Myrtle May would get a big kick out of that, giggling and carrying on the whole time Annabelle munched down on the carrot. I'd gotten so I'd always bring some rock candy along that your Grandmamma Hixie made out of sorghum. Your grandmamma was Mose's daughter, and I ended up marrying her just after I turned eighteen. Kind of strange that I married the daughter of the man that killed Daddy, I reckon, but I never had no ill will toward Mose. He was a good man.

And besides, it hadn't been his fault.

Anyway, I kept that candy folded up in my hanky, and I'd always open it up for her before I got started on Dr. Love's privy. I'll never forget those little hands, white and creamy as goat's milk, reaching into my hanky, rooting around for the biggest piece. She always wanted me to eat a little with her.

"Ain't you gonna have a piece, Jim Limey?"

"No, Miss Myrtle May, I don't reckon I will."

"Please have just one square with me," she'd say, and then I'd go ahead and have a piece. It was like a little game we always played. Then I'd get to work and that smell from the privy would directly drive her away.

Even though I only charged a nickel for my work, Dr. Love always gave me fifteen cents. Every time. And at Christmas he'd slide me an extra dollar. Tell me to buy something nice for Mama. I got her a brass picture frame that first year and stuck Daddy's picture in it—the only one she had, which she kept tacked to the wall above her bed. It was a good picture too, of him wearing his favorite floppy hat and smiling wide. I set it by her little bedside table so it was the first thing she saw on Christmas morning. She come into the kitchen just a boo-hooing, squeezing that frame to her chest, giving me a bear-hug so tight she nearly choked the breath out of me. I think there were some happy tears mixed in with all those sad ones though, because she smiled and her eyes said thank you. Nearly got me to crying, seeing Mama like that, knowing how much she missed Daddy.

I can recollect the day he died like it was yesterday.

Got knocked upside the head with a baseball bat and it killed him dead on the spot. Deader than a sack of hammers. Like I said before, it was ol' Mose that did it to him. He and Daddy and Rufus Cupp and Bigbad were playing ball one Saturday evening with another team of Negroes from the neighboring town of Pittman's Corner. That's what they always did, played baseball every Saturday except when it got too cold sometimes in the winter. They'd get stewed like witches, drinking corn liquor and chewing plugs of tobacco. Had themselves a big time.

That particular evening, Daddy and the others were in a tight game while all the ladies sat around in the bleachers, gossiping. I was playing mumblety-peg in the vacant lot next to the church with my little brothers. I remember turning toward the ballfield when Bigbad yelled for Daddy to clobber one. Daddy was a hell of a good hitter, and I always liked watching him play.

I saw Daddy all bent down, brushing away the grit that covered the plate—in this case a flattened pie tin. As he settled into his stance, wiggling his feet into the sandy soil, Mose stood off to the side, in what today would be called the on-deck circle. Mose was practicing his swing when—Mama later blamed it on the hooch, and I reckon she was right—that bat slipped right out of his sweaty hands and whirly-birded straight at Daddy's head.

Mose was the best player out of all of them. He had himself a pretty swing that flowed naturally. He always hit more homers than any of the others, even Daddy. But on this evening, his bat connected with the soft spot on the side of Daddy's skull instead of a baseball. Daddy dropped, his face full of sand, dead just that quick. At least he didn't suffer none. Mama suffered something fierce.

Well, anyways, one day a bunch of years later—it was October 8th, that I know for sure—I'd headed to town on privy duty. I remember the day exactly because me and Hixie had been married for two years that day and she'd pestered me to stay home. Just like a woman, using all those tricks you women use, keeping us men from doing our jobs. But I told her I had to get on. It took everything I had in me to fight her off, too, because I was still a young jackrabbit back then and Hixie was an eye-popper if there ever was one. But I went on, telling her I'd try and get home early if I could manage. Well, I managed it all right, but not the way I'd planned.

The first sign I had that something wasn't right was when I saw ol' nutty Caledonia in the street, mumbling something or other. Caledonia was a big, heavy woman and crazy as a coot. She used to keep house for some of the white folks until she went loony. She always walked around wearing a dirty dress and carrying a straw broom, sweeping pine needles and pine cones. But she never did sweep the sidewalk or the street; she only swept the yard, in winter just as likely as summer. And not just in front of her house, in front of every dern house in Weems, talking to herself all the while. I couldn't ever understand a word she said. All the children, colored and white, they were more scared of her than any haint that might have been floating around in the woods.

I knew something was off when she stopped sweeping and looked up at Miss Annabelle and me when we come rolling into Weems. Caledonia always kept her head down and didn't pay no mind to anyone that come by, like she was off in her own place somewhere. But this time she looked up at me and spoke clear as day. "It's a dark time, Jim Limey. Dark as death and there ain't no hope." I didn't know what the devil Caledonia was talking about, but it scared me bad. I didn't even know she knew my name, seeing as how she'd never spoken a direct word to me before. But there she was, talking about death and darkness. It sent a chill running up and down my arms, standing my little hairs on end. I snapped the reins and Miss Annabelle broke into a trot, which must have meant she was scared too, because she didn't ever go no faster than a blind turtle for nobody.

I made my first couple of stops and that's when I got my second sign: there wasn't a soul at home at any of the places I went to. And then it hit me after my fourth or fifth stop that I hadn't seen anyone walking on the streets either, other than Caledonia. When I rounded the corner in the square, heading for Dr. Love's house, that's when I knew something bad had happened. The sheriff's prowler was in the driveway and there were a mess of people standing around talking to each other, no voice above a whisper. I stopped when I spotted Bigbad in the crowd—it wasn't hard to do, him being a whole head taller than any other man in Weems—and he come over and told me everything.

"Miss Myrtle May gone missing," he said. "They cain't find her nowhere."

My heart just about fell out of my chest when Bigbad said that.

"They said there ain't no trace of her. It's like she plum disappeared."

I sensed something in the air, the same way you feel a storm coming in off the ocean, and I think every one of those folks standing around felt it, too. I decided I'd head on home, not feeling much like working. I knew Hixie would be all excited when I pulled up, thinking I come back early for a little coitus, but that wouldn't last once I told the news. Trying to explain it to Hixie, that's what I was thinking about when I noticed someone other than Bigbad next to my wagon.

"Hey, boy, I'm talking to you."

Wendell Burroughs stared at me, his eyes sharp and squinted like a snake's.

"Did you hear me?" he said quietly, as if he didn't want no one to hear him talking to me. His face looked weak, tired. "Don't be going by my place today, you hear? Under the circumstances and all."

"Yes, sir. Okay. That's what I was just thinking to myself. That I ought to go on home."

"You just come on by tomorrow. And make sure you bring me plenty of lime," he said. "I'm nearly out."

"You're out, Mr. Burroughs?" I said. "I just refilled your bucket last week."

"Just bring some, boy," he said, mean and nasty as ever. "Don't you know to stay out of a white man's business? You best be careful, understand?"

And I understood, all right. I understood exactly. I got real scared then, not because of what he said, but because of what I knew. Caledonia's words, the feeling in the air, Wendell Burroughs needing lime. It just all come together. Like Jesus whispered it in my ear. And Wendell Burroughs standing in that crowd all cool and calm like he was just as worried about Myrtle May as the rest of us. Sickened me, is what it did. And all those folks, including Dr. Love and the sheriff, having no idea.

"Yes, sir," I replied. "I'll bring some by tomorrow." Then I popped the reins and got on out of there. On the way home, my body shook worse than a dog afflicted.

Next morning I still felt sick, like I'd been in the corn liquor. I didn't want to go over to Wendell Burroughs's place, not for nothing, but I didn't want to cross him just then. No telling what he might do. Besides, I still didn't know for certain if he'd guiltied himself. Hixie begged me to stay home. She was scared for me ever since I told her about Caledonia and all the signs and what I'd felt in my bones. She stuck two dried cattails into a pair of Coke bottles and lit them. They were smoking on the front porch when I left, warding off the evil.

A grassy lane ran the back part of Dr. Love's property, leading to Wendell Burroughs's place, and I steered Miss Annabelle under the limbs of the walnut trees to get there. I wasn't for sure what might happen, though I did feel a bit better when I saw the sheriff's prowler in the driveway, same as the day before. I wanted to yell for the sheriff to follow me because I thought I knew who done it. But it was just like what Wendell Burroughs had said—I knew better than to fool in a white man's business, no matter the circumstances. If I accused him of taking Myrtle May and it turned out I was wrong, I'd be swinging in the Hanging Woods by nightfall. I wasn't going to take that chance, not even for little Myrtle May.

When I showed up, everything was quiet and still, the only noise the cardinals and catbirds singing in the morning sunshine. It was a pretty day, felt real nice, like that humidity had finally decided to up and leave and wouldn't be back until spring. Floating in the breeze was that good smell of fresh-turned crops.

Wendell Burroughs's house appeared closed-up and dark. I hoped he was either sleeping or out working. I slid off the wagon seat and went to the privy to grab his bucket. When I opened the door, I got the Holy Jesus scared out of me because Wendell Burroughs was in there. I smacked him with the door and he screamed out. I always made a habit of knocking before I went in, but my mind was so filled up with Myrtle May that I forgot. I stepped back and he come out a second later, gimping on that bum leg, his face white as the lime I'd brought. When he saw it was me, though, it went angry red.

"Goddamnit, nigger, don't you know to knock before you open a Johnny-house. Stupid sonovabitch. Almost give me a heart attack."

My whole body shook. "I'm awfully sorry, Mr.

Burroughs," I said, dropping my head. "Just wanted to get your bucket filled up. Then I was fixing to clean out that hole. Figured you was still sleeping."

"Well, I ain't sleeping, boy. And I decided I ain't gonna be needing you to clean out the hole no more. Just fill up my pail."

He went inside the privy and come out with the bucket. I filled it at the wagon and carried it back over, but he blocked me from taking it inside.

"I'll do it," he said, grabbing the bucket. He dumped the entire thing down the hole, then handed it back. "Give me one more. Shoot, I don't know why I been paying you to do this. I can do it just as easy."

"Usually, Mr. Burroughs, I only dump a few scoops in at a time, not the whole thing like that."

Soon as I said it, I wished I hadn't. He stepped up and put his nose to where it almost touched mine. Would have, too, if I hadn't been wearing my brimmed hat. The whiskey on his breath nearly got my own head abuzzing. "I thought I told you yesterday to stay out of a white man's business. Ain't that what I told you?"

"Yes, sir, that's right. And I'm sorry. I'll get you another bucketful."

"You're sorry all right," he said.

I brought him one more, then got on my seat, ready to skedaddle. He reached into the pocket of his overalls, pulled out two dimes, handed them to me. I wasn't expecting that, I'll tell you.

"You come back in a few days with more lime," he said. "If I ain't here just leave it. Pay you when I see you.

But I don't want you messing with that hole. You understand?"

"Yes, sir. I understand," I said. And then I got out of there. I hadn't been certain before, but I was sure enough certain by then.

The rest of the morning, as I cleaned out the other privies around town, I couldn't think about nothing but Myrtle May. It bothered me something fierce, knowing that the lime I produced with my own hands was the very thing covering her up, keeping the sheriff from finding her.

Now, this last part I'm about to tell you, I ain't never uttered it to nobody before. Not even your grandmamma. Reckon I've been ashamed all these years. Or just too scared. When Hixie was dying, I wanted to tell her, just so there wouldn't have been no secrets between us, but it would've only killed her that much faster. I'm an old man now, had a good life I reckon, and I know just as well as you that this cancer's got me good. Figured I better admit to someone before I die, just so I'd have a clear mind when I go to meet Jesus.

Myrtle May never was found. Nobody arrested for it or nothing. Only me and Hixie and Wendell Burroughs, I reckon, ever knew the truth about where Myrtle May really was. As the years went by and flush toilets became more popular, I guess you could say my business went down the drain. Dr. Love was one of the first to get a flush toilet, but I didn't blame him none. I'd have probably had me one down at my place, too, if I could've afforded it.

I'd see Dr. Love outside in the yard sometimes when I'd go past. He'd never been the same after Myrtle May disappeared. I don't reckon nobody ever is, losing a child that way, with no answers. Always wondering. He'd stare at his crepe myrtles, trimming them here or there, but he didn't ever seem to be on this Earth no more. Like Caledonia, off in his own place.

Wendell Burroughs couldn't afford a flush toilet, so he still had me come every week with the lime, but he never did have me clean out his privy for him again. One day I went out there to drop off a bucketful. This was years after Myrtle May disappeared. I had a bunch of children of my own by then, including your daddy. Anyway, I went out there and stopped where I always did, beneath them walnuts. It was early morning, midsummer, barely light out. When I got off the wagon, I looked back and saw tracks in the grass where my wheels had gone through the dew. Kind of sparkling, the grass was, with that morning sunshine lighting it up.

I went to the privy and filled up his bucket. I ain't going to lie neither, I always peeked down that hole, just wondering if I might see something—a shoe, a speck of dress, that little baby doll she used to carry, something. It was always too dark, but I looked anyway. Well, I come out of there and was heading to the wagon when I heard a noise. Sounded like a boar hog rutting with a sow, but not nearly as loud. Just a soft grunt really.

I turned toward the house, trying to see if I might hear it again. And then I did. I started creeping up real slow, like a cat on a bird, waiting to see if I'd hear it again, trying to pinpoint exactly where it come from. And then I saw him, Wendell Burroughs, down at the bottom of those steep, rickety stairs, his body all twisted up like a stubborn yew root, his legs in the bushes. His head rested on a slate steppingstone, a stream of dried blood on it, running off into the yard. I stood over him as the sun got a little higher, coming up over the trees. Glass glistened all around, same as that morning dew had done. Then I glimpsed the broken handle from a whiskey jug on the bottom step, and a few more pieces higher up the stairs, like a little trail left behind as he'd tumbled.

"You all right, Mr. Burroughs?" I said. "You need some help?"

His head stayed on that stone and his eyes looked up at me, his neck turned all crooked and uncomfortable like. He didn't move none, except his mouth, trying to say something. But nothing come out but another of those grunts. His lips twitched a little, reminding me of a banked catfish that had swallowed a hook deep. And this part I'll never forget. His tongue was whiter than a cottonmouth's, his eyes bloodshot and swollen. A real sight, he was. Looked like to me he'd probably been out there a couple days already, baking in the sun like an autumn fox-grape left too long on the vine.

"I sure am sorry, Mr. Burroughs," I said, "but I can't understand you. And I know better'n to fool in a white man's business."

That's when I got on my wagon and left. I've always felt guilty about it, ashamed to no end. Not one day's gone by since then that I didn't think about Wendell

Burroughs. But it was me or him, and I chose me.

There ain't no good that comes from letting something suffer, whether it's an animal, a man, or even Wendell Burroughs, I reckon. There ain't nothing good about keeping something locked up inside you for that long neither. So that's why I had to tell somebody, because I wanted to get everything straight down here before I headed on up to the next place. I reckon Jesus would want it that way. And I'll be honest, the way I see it, Wendell Burroughs got his due. That ain't the way of Jesus, I know, but somehow I hope He'll forgive me. Figure we'll probably have a long talk about it before He lets me through the gates for good.

Only God knows if I did the right thing or not. But I left him, spread out in his yard with that sun coming up, and I could tell it was going to be another hot one. A real scorcher. And it was, too.

Joyride

My mother bit her nails continuously during the trip to Rahway State Prison. She kept looking in the rear-view, too, not to check her hair or apply lipstick like she usually did when driving, but instead to see behind us. Almost like she was worried somebody might be following.

"When we pick him up," she said, "I need you to hop in the back. I want to be able to keep my eyes on him."

"Okay, Ma, but geez, it's just Mickey. You're acting like he's some crazy murderer or something."

"Prison changes people," she said. "And never for the better." She adjusted the paisley headscarf knotted beneath her chin, then slid her oversized sunglasses down her nose to make eye contact. "I made a promise to Suzie, God rest her soul. And as her sister, I'm obliged to keep that promise. But that doesn't mean I have to like it."

That promise. That damned promise my mother was always talking about. *Blood is thicker than water,* she'd sometimes mutter. *Her last dying wish* other times. I'd heard it for the past six months, ever since Aunt Suzie, at only forty-one, died from lupus. The promise ticked me off, mainly because I thought it was selfish on Suzie's part. I hadn't been in that hospital room, but I imagined the scene well enough. My mother squeezing Suzie's hand as she lay on the bed, breathing her last phlegmy breaths. "Take care of Mickey when he's released, Meredith. Promise me you'll look after him."

One night, after Ma had a few too many Schaefers, she went on a rant. "Suzie might as well have said, 'Meredith, I need you to babysit my pet rattlesnake. He's very sweet and gentle but grossly misunderstood. Just don't do anything to startle or upset him and you'll be fine.'"

As Ma turned onto the prison road, she suddenly came to a dead stop. She wore driving gloves, and the leather fingers squeezed the oversized wheel of the Mercury in anticipation. "He's right down there, Charlie," she said. "See him?"

An image from one of the many Westerns I watched each weekend at the movie-house flashed in my head, the showdown at high noon about to take place on the barren street. "Yeah, I see him."

"Already released and waiting for us."

At the end of the block, leaning against a telephone pole, was Mickey. No mistaking it. He wasn't tall—I was only fifteen, yet already a head higher—but he was strong and wide. Broad shoulders stretched his black jacket as if the leather was his actual skin. His dark hair was slicked back with grease. Mickey took a swig from a bottle wrapped in a brown bag as smoke curled around his opposite hand. His jerky movements and mannerisms made him appear upset about being late for a rumble or something.

Ma exhaled then drove forward, slowly creeping to the corner. Mickey kicked at something on the sidewalk, a rock or bottle cap maybe, and as we approached, whatever it was zinged across the road where the mouth of a sewer grate swallowed it.

My window was down, and both the cool air and the stink of the town were a bit overwhelming. "Hey, Charlie, how's it going, pal?" said Mickey with a smile. His teeth were white and perfect. He'd always been nothing but nice and friendly to me. Charming even. He seemed content, as if he'd been standing on that street corner each and every day, just watching the cars pass, instead of being locked up in Jersey's toughest prison for the last year. He put his palms on the door and leaned in, oblivious to the drifting, choking smoke. "Hey, Aunt Mer. Sure appreciate the lift. And nice wheels. Always loved me a Mercury."

Behind him, the cold dead façade of the prison loomed. Tall, ugly vegetation with wiry tendrils had woven its way through gaps in the fencing. Stray newspaper stuck to parts of the chain-link, as if someone had begun a wallpaper job they gave up on. That fencing, topped with strands of barbwire, encompassed the entire town it seemed. For blocks and blocks it went, standing in stark contrast to the brightness and zeal of Mickey.

He took one last swig before heaving the bottle in the general direction of the prison, grinning when the glass smashed against the cracked, weed-choked pavement of an abandoned parking lot.

"How are you, Mickey?" said Ma. Her voice might have quivered.

Mickey tapped the end of his cigarette, ridding it of ash, and appeared to ruminate deeply about Ma's question, as if he hadn't understood it was simply standard salutation. "I'm behind," he said, giving a slight nod as if to emphasize his seriousness. "So far behind I think I'm in front." And then he laughed good-naturedly as he winked at me.

In the car, it didn't take him long to open up. Per Ma's instructions, I'd tried to get out and jump into the backseat but he put a stop to that. He insisted on being in back, not wanting to disrupt me or my mother any more than he already had. Ma slid her sunglasses down her nose again and gave me a long, cold, disappointed stare. *One job,* her gaze seemed to say. *I gave you one job and you failed.*

"I mean, when I went into the clink everything was hunky-dory, you know? Thirteen months later and the world's turned to shit," he said before leaning forward over the seat partition with a genuine look of regret. "Pardon my language, Aunt Mer. You pick up bad habits on the inside."

Ma shrugged as she eyed the mirror, his entire face, big as life, staring back at her and blocking the view. "It's okay, Mickey. I understand."

"Thirteen months, you know, and now everything's different. Ma's dead and they wouldn't even let me see her. Won't ever forgive the bastards for that. Never. And then some nut shoots our President while he's sitting in a goddamned convertible? What's that all about? Oh, and now a bunch of guys my age are in some Chink country I've never heard of getting blown to shit? Sorry again, Aunt Mer. I mean, what the hell happened?"

An hour later we arrived home to our little town of Bartley, a different world entirely compared to the grittiness of Rahway. The plan was for Mickey to stay in our guestroom until he found a job, got on his feet, and secured an apartment. After all, he was only nineteen. Recently motherless, always fatherless. And Ma had made that promise.

He had no bag or suitcase, no possessions. He'd gone inside quickly, examined the room, then met us in the kitchen. "I'm gonna walk down to the bar and knock a few back. See if I can find any of the old crew. I'll slip in later, Aunt Mer. Don't wait up."

Ma fidgeted, grabbing a dishrag from the oven door and nervously twisting it. I wondered right then how different she might have acted if my father was still around. Would she be more relaxed? More at ease? It didn't matter, since he'd long ago made it clear he wasn't coming back.

"I don't have a spare key," she said, almost in apology. "I'll leave mine under the mat."

Mickey shook his head emphatically, went toward the window, put his fingers on the sill, and rubbed lightly as if in deep study. "No, Aunt Mer. No, no, no. You put it under the mat and you're just inviting hoods like me to come on in and take everything you got. Go ahead and lock her up tight."

"But how will—"

"I'll get in, don't worry," he said as he winked at me again. There was something about that wink that made me proud right then. As if I was in on his little secret. As if I was now a part of his underground gang. I suddenly liked the idea of having a man in the house, even if he was only four years my senior. Part father, part brother, part cousin, who'd spent over a year in prison for B&E. He was tough, and I liked tough.

As instructed, Ma locked the house up tight. When I got up for school the next morning, I glanced into the guestroom as I passed. It smelled of smoke and stale liquor, and sure enough, Mickey was tucked beneath the covers, sleeping soundly. I got the distinct impression that the normal rules of the world didn't apply to him. He understood them, recognized they existed, he just didn't bother to adhere. It was so different from what I was used to, from how I'd been raised, but I liked it. Admired it even.

When Mickey was fourteen, he'd been kicked out of public school for beating up his science teacher. Had pummeled the man with his fists, then smashed a beaker across his forehead because he'd gotten an F on a quiz. One measly quiz. Mickey had been sent off to reform school in Montclair and had only grown harder while there. Apparently, reform school hadn't done much in the way of reforming. After his stint, he'd regularly been in and out of jail, not to mention his most recent stay in prison.

But in the six months since we'd picked him up, Mickey appeared to be on the straight and narrow, working for a moving company. He came and went as he pleased, sometimes away for days, then popping back in again, often dressed in new clothes or with a different car. He'd have one vehicle, then after only a few weeks—or sometimes days—he'd trade it in for something else. "I like to keep it fresh, you know? I get bored easy." That was Mickey. And I have to admit, he'd caused no problems for me or Ma. In fact, he'd started paying rent without being prompted. One day he just handed her some cash and had continued each month ever since. And God knows we needed it. That money, no doubt, helped soften Ma a bit.

So when he asked her if I could join him on a job, her arm hadn't needed much twisting. Summer had started, I'd turned sixteen, and I was itching to make some money. Plus, I was excited to spend time with Mickey, away from Ma's watchful eyes.

"Boss needs some extra bodies for a bit we're doing in Jersey City," he'd told her. "Moving an AT&T office building: desks, chairs, the whole shebang. Charlie'll make nearly four bucks an hour."

We'd driven off the next morning in a Ford Falcon he'd brought home two days earlier. I was thrilled, but it didn't take long to realize we wouldn't be moving any office furniture that day. Or ever. Instead, Mickey had driven forty minutes due east from Bartley, straight over the George Washington, exited onto Jerome Avenue, and presto, we were in the gritty underbelly of the South Bronx. But I hadn't been scared or worried. Not as long as I was with Mickey. If Mickey was with you, the only thing you had to fear was...well, Mickey himself. People crossed to the opposite sidewalk when they saw him coming. He had a swagger, a hardness, which most rational folks immediately recognized: steer clear of that guy. The hackles of dogs would stand on end when he passed. But for me, just being around him made me feel tough, as if toughness was contagious. Made me walk with confidence. Made me invincible.

Mickey skillfully maneuvered the car through side streets, cutting underneath a set of suspended train tracks. Red lights didn't generally apply to him. Stop signs were optional. He worked his way into the dark netherworld of the interior South Bronx where stripped and burned-out cars lined the streets, where stacks of trash and ripped sofas were piled on sidewalks, where the only white face I saw was Mickey's. When he pulled into an alley, weaving and dodging around dumpsters and dented garbage cans, and then stopped at a corrugated steel door, I was absolutely positive I wouldn't find any office furniture on the other side. I didn't know what Mickey was up to, but I knew for sure it had nothing to do with loading a van with chairs and desks and typewriters.

"Jump out and pound on the door four times. Like this," said Mickey as he slapped the dashboard *bam...*

ba-bam-bam. "Then get your ass back in the car."

I looked at him with wide eyes, then out at my surroundings. It was late morning, but in the dark alley between the apartment buildings, it might as well have been night. Directly next to the garage door was a dumpster, overflowing with garbage, and as I exited, I knew someone was going to jump out and beat me senseless. "Are you serious?" I said.

"As a heart attack. You're gonna make some big loot today."

"What're we doing?"

"We're moving stuff," said Mickey, a cigarette in his lips as he gave me his signature wink, his right eyelid hanging droopily where he'd been on the wrong end of a powerful fist during reform school. The owner of that fist, I imagined, even meaner and tougher than Mickey. "I told your ma we're in the moving business and I didn't lie. I'm gonna teach you a trade. Something useful. Now go, I don't got all day."

I ran to the door and slammed the side of my fist against the steel ridges, mimicking the beat Mickey had tapped out. On my return, I slipped in a puddle of tepid, black grease-water, and my body sprawled out, front-side, when I hit the ground. The smell was putrid, and I gagged as I stood up, dripping with muck.

"Just follow me in," yelled Mickey through the window as the mysterious garage door rose, clanging and echoing down the alley. He was laughing. "You look like a horse just shit on your face."

I flicked my hands and wiped them on the butt of my

jeans. I was scared, yes, but also exhilarated. I had no idea what was in store, had no idea what illegal underworld hid behind that door, but a sense of toughness raced through me as I walked into a fully functioning garage.

Mickey stopped the car and got out. A cacophony deafened me: welders and grinders, metal banging against metal, the clanging of hammers on steel, the garage door closing behind. Pieces of cars lay scattered about. Quarter panels, windshields, wheels and tires, engine blocks suspended with heavy chains from steel girders. Car parts were stowed in every available corner as a half-dozen men, all dark-skinned Italians, dismantled the vehicles. It was all a wonder.

"Who the hell is this?" said a guy, yelling over the noise. He was short and built like a whiskey barrel, his forearms larger than my calves. A dark, fluffy mustache hung on his upper lip, and it wiggled as he spoke. He got right in Mickey's face. "What're ya bringing a kid for?"

"He's my cousin," said Mickey, not shying away. "He'll be good. Gonna show him the ropes tonight."

"I don't need no kid lifting cars. I told you that upfront. I got enough lifters as is. Get him the hell out. You bring him back, I'll put a tire iron to your skull." He shoved a thick pointer finger into Mickey's chest. "I'll take this one," he said, gesturing toward the Falcon, "since it's already here. Two hundred."

"Two-fifty," said Mickey. "Gotta give the kid something. Got this one in Jersey. She's clean as a whistle."

The mustached man walked away and entered a glassed-in cubicle. The other men never even looked at us as they worked. When he came back, he dragged a garbage bag across the sawdusted floor. "Here's two-twenty-five," he said. "The extra's for dumping these plates. But at least three blocks away. You got me?"

"I got you, Lou," said Mickey as he pocketed the cash. "Anything you're looking for in particular? We're gonna hit midtown. Be back tonight with whatever you want."

"Are you goddamned deaf?" said Lou. "I said no kids. Now get outta here while you're still breathing. And clean this punk up, for Christ's sake. Stinks like a pig's asshole." Lou reached for a rag resting on the rungs of an extension ladder and tossed it, hitting me squarely in the chest. I wiped the black grime from my hands and face.

"Thunderbird? One of those little Corvette Sharks? Whatever you want, just tell me."

Lou shook his head but offered the slightest smile. "You don't quit, do you? But that's why I like you, Mick. You got fire. The fire of a devil. Late fifties T-birds are always in demand," said Lou as he turned and yelled at one of his men to move the Falcon.

Mickey said to me, "Grab that bag. Let's go." He pulled the rope of the garage door, cracking it half-way. I ducked as I dragged the heavy license plates behind me, like a rogue Santa with an illegal pack of goods. And it did feel like Christmas in a way. Some sort of delinquent, sinister Christmas. I smiled from ear to ear.

* * *

On the bus ride into Manhattan, Mickey gave vague instructions. "But nothing's set in stone," he said. "That's why it's exciting. Different every time. Never know what you're gonna get into."

We wandered down to Washington Square Park and spent the day and early evening sitting on a bench drinking from Schlitz Tall Boys. Other than stealing a few sips from my mother's Schaeffers, I'd never drank alcohol. So by the time I'd downed thirty-two ounces of malt liquor, I had quite a zipping buzz. I felt good, watching throngs of people stroll in the warm summer evening, tourists taking pictures in front of the grand arch, college girls strutting by in skirts. I felt alive. Like I was starting to find my way in the world.

"Come on, let's go," said Mickey.

He walked down the sidewalk with his hands stuffed into his denim jacket, his chest out, his mannerisms confident. I did my best to keep up, trying to look tough, or as tough as a baby-faced sixteen-year-old, stained with grease and grime, could look. Teenaged girls and full adult women glanced at Mickey, a combination of fear, intrigue, and desire glazing their eyes. If the entire world was a black-and-white photograph, Mickey was a bright red spot smack in the middle of that picture, demanding attention. I realized, right then and there, I wanted people to look at me that way someday, too.

We walked up 6th Avenue, then headed west on 11th, Mickey keeping his head on a subtle swivel as he scanned the street. Just after we'd crossed the Bleecker intersection, Mickey suddenly stopped. "Come here," he said, sitting me down on the front stoop of a brownstone. The street was dark, and we were nearly impossible to see.

"Look over there, about eight cars down," he whispered as he removed a pack of cigarettes. He rolled a Zippo over his leg and lit up, the sweet smell of tobacco shrouding us. To my surprise, he handed me the lighter. "You see it?"

I looked through the haze of smoke and darkness, eyeing the parked cars that all appeared more-or-less the same in the shadows. "I'm not sure," I said. "Which one?"

"Two cars before that payphone on the corner. A red T-bird. Looks like a fifty-eight," he said as a passing truck's headlights brushed over the side door. "Sitting there like a hot apple-pie in Granny's windowsill."

"Yeah, I see it," I said, the beer in my head still working. "Is that the one?"

"That's the one." His cigarette glowed in the darkness as he took a heavy draw. "We'll cross over, and you just walk around to the passenger side, cool as can be. Got me? Like you're waiting for me to get in and unlock your door. Don't look around. Don't say nothing. Just stand there. Shouldn't take thirty seconds. That's a five hundred buck score from Lou, easy. When I give the word, you'll spark that lighter so I can see."

Mickey flicked away his cigarette, then we crossed. I stuffed my fingers into my jeans pockets, trying to remain cool, but my chest pounded. My cheeks prickled with heat. I glanced over when Mickey casually reached inside his jacket and pulled out a metal object, about the size of a ruler.

"Eyes forward, shithead," he whispered. "What'd I tell you?"

When Mickey paused at the rear bumper, I cut behind it to the passenger door, feeling like a scolded puppy. He approached the driver's side, tried the handle, but it failed to open. He slid the object against the window and pushed downward quickly with both hands as if churning butter. Immediately there was a faint *click*. He opened the door calmly and a second later I slid into the front seat.

"Spark the lighter," whispered Mickey with an urgent edge.

I did so.

"Hold it down here a little," he said, now hunched forward, his hands beneath the dashboard.

I leaned in with the Zippo, offering more light. Mickey jerked and suddenly held a ball of wires in both hands as if he'd just ripped the guts out of a fish. His fingers moved with expertise and dexterity as he muddled through the wires, finding the pair he wanted. He pinched them in his fingers, then procured a small pocketknife so quickly that I hadn't even seen him do it. He shaved off the casings, exposing shiny copper wires, touched the tips as a few sparks flew, and suddenly the powerful engine of the Thunderbird roared to life. The engine revved as Mickey worked the gas pedal. He put the car in gear, looked over his shoulder, and pulled out smoothly, heading for the West Side Highway. All told, from the time we'd first approached until we pulled away from the sidewalk, had taken less than two minutes. But a scream from behind dropped my heart straight into my ballsack. "Hey, you son of a bitch, that's my car."

A man ran down the middle of the street, his tie flapping behind him like a cape, his arms waving. Mickey laughed, watching the frantic man in the rear-view. "That's what insurance is for, pal." And then in his best carnie voice, "Everybody's a winnaaah."

Mickey raced in and out of traffic, slipping by cars and taxis as if he did it every day. And, I started to realize, he probably did. Mickey had one hand on the wheel and a cigarette in the other, looking over his shoulder as he shot into another lane.

All sorts of confusing things spun through my head. The beer for one. Excitement and adrenaline for another. Mickey had given me twenty dollars earlier for dumping the license plates, and he'd promised another fifty for simply holding a lighter. By the time summer was over, I realized, I could be rich. Very rich.

As the Thunderbird roared down the highway, as taillights passed my peripheral in blurry red streaks, I envisioned all the things I'd buy, most notably my own car. I'd be the coolest kid in school. My friends and I could go to the drive-in with any girls we wanted, maybe even the best-looking seniors. But despite the alcohol and fantasy, I also felt guilt. What would my mother say? She'd be crushed, knowing her son had followed in Mickey's footsteps. And to add to the nauseating roil now in my gut, I believed every bright light I saw was a cop getting ready to arrest us.

For the next month and a half, I'd go with Mickey three or four times a week. Sometimes we'd lift in the city, sometimes in Jersey. It just depended on what we spotted. And I'd developed quite an eye for not only picking out targets, but also seeing the bigger picture, notably escape routes and potential problems. "You've caught on fast, Charlie. Hell, you're almost ready to do it on your own."

I didn't know about that, though the idea intrigued me. I could hot-wire now. Or simply use a screwdriver. He'd shown me how to master the Slim Jim. I knew the routes. I understood the game. As we raced through the night in a '63 Impala we'd just clipped from a garage in Washington Heights, I fantasized about striking out on my own. About how Lou would pay me directly instead of just getting the scraps Mickey threw my way.

We were only three blocks from the chop-shop when Mickey took a corner too fast, trying to beat a red light. A Negro woman was crossing at the intersection, her thickly braided hair wrapped atop her head like a coiled snake, her bright dress a patchwork of reds and greens and blacks. She seemed to glimmer with life beneath a streetlamp.

What I heard first was the squealing of tires, a piercing sound that ripped through the quiet and empty streets. I instinctively reached for the giant dashboard, bracing for impact. The woman looked up, directly at Mickey and me, a broad white smile disappearing into the darkest face I'd ever seen. *From a different country*, I thought in that brief instant. *Maybe somewhere in Africa.* A pretty face. Smooth, perfect skin. That is, it was smooth and perfect until the front bumper smashed into her knees, taking her legs out and launching her into flight. Her bag of groceries hit the hood first, followed directly by that pretty face. That pretty face quickly turning ghastly as it slid across the hulking steel hood, then collided with the windshield. Coming directly at me like she wanted to deliver a fat kiss. Then her body, wrapped in the vibrant colors of her dress, rolled off the car and into the street as Mickey violently turned the wheel.

The car slid across the intersection and smashed into the steel pole holding the traffic signal. My chin collided with the dashboard, and I instantly tasted a splash of blood. Mickey's face, after it slammed the large steering wheel, looked as bad as the woman's.

"Get out of here," gargled Mickey through blood and pieces of teeth. "Run."

I stayed right where I was, not moving. My hands trembled, and when I looked down at them, my fingernails were tearing into the upholstery.

"I said run. Get the hell out of here." A column of blood flowed from Mickey's forehead, rolling straight down the bridge of his nose, over his lips, and then dripping from his chin.

I ran like hell. I had no idea where to go, no idea where I was, but I started running, directly down the middle of the street, leaping over dented canned goods, then passing right by the woman who was outstretched in the intersection, her one arm pointing straight up in the air as if frozen and reaching out to God.

Already people poured from their apartment buildings, and I distinctly heard the voice of a woman, a Negro woman it sounded like, yell, "He's getting away. That one's getting away."

I sprinted for what seemed like hours, having no idea of what I should do or where I should go. But I kept moving, not remembering exactly how I managed to do what I did, but by the time the sun came up, I found myself in the High Bridge train station in Jersey, less than fifteen miles from home. I hitched a ride from there and walked into an empty house, Ma already having left for work, a note on the counter saying she loved me and there were leftovers in the fridge.

For the next couple of days, I wasn't able to sleep. Or eat. Or do anything really. Every time I heard a sound outside I worried it was the cops surrounding the house. If a siren wailed in town, I knew they were coming for me. Mickey hadn't shown up, and I didn't know if he was in jail or not, alive or not. I had no idea and I didn't care. I wanted nothing to do with him. Actually, that's not entirely true. If I'm completely honest, a part of me missed him. Missed the excitement. The thrill. The companionship.

It was three days later when I found out that the woman had been from Jamaica, having moved to the States only two years before with her baby daughter. A daughter who, now five years old, was a ward of the state. I learned all of this from a bruised and battered Mickey, who popped in through a locked bathroom window while I was eating breakfast. "I got away before the cops showed. Had to punch through an angry crowd, but they backed off after I throttled the first couple guys."

"So, she's dead?" I said. "Jesus."

"Yeah, it's a shame," he said. Several of his bottom teeth were missing, making him look even more intimidating. "But it's part of the game, you know?"

Despite knowing better, knowing I should have told Ma everything, should have called the cops, I found myself nodding. "But her kid," I finally managed. "I mean, she's an orphan now."

"Shit, I'm an orphan, too. She's an orphan, I'm an orphan. Big deal."

"She's five years old, Mick. You were like seventeen or something."

"I've managed okay. She'll figure it out."

He looked away then, and instantly I realized he hadn't meant it. His voice had broken ever so slightly. He was bothered. And in that moment, everything changed. It was like some weird sort of clarity settled in.

"Hell, what do you want me to do?" he continued

though he wouldn't look at me. Instead, he stared out the window at a robin hopping along in the grass. "We can't go back in time. What's done is done. The lady's dead, I hit her, end of story. And how's me going back to prison gonna change things? Will that bring her back to life? Is her kid gonna have a mamma again?"

"No, I guess not," I said. I stared out the window now too, somber, watching the robin poke for a worm or whatever it is they eat in the early morning. I knew what had to be done now. Everything was making sense.

"Exactly. End of conversation, then. So we lay low for a good long while. Hell, maybe I'll get me a straight job. Give that a whirl. Shoot, you'll be back in school before—"

"No!" I said, louder than I'd anticipated. Mickey, startled, whipped his head around to look at me as I continued. "Hell, no, we're not laying low."

"What?"

"I got my eye on a pretty baby blue Corvette," I said, now staring at the homemade stitches laced like a zipper across his forehead. "Saw it parked over by the deli last night. It's time to get back to work."

For a second, and it was only a second, but in that instant I saw Mickey hesitate, as if he wasn't exactly sure who he was dealing with. "Yeah, sure. Okay," he said, and for the first time he smiled. He gave me a little punch on the shoulder, as if that sealed our bond. A father might've mussed his kid's hair, acquaintances might've shaken hands, but Mickey, my cousin Mickey, he punched me. And that meant everything. "What time you wanna hit it?"

"Tonight," I said. "Soon as it's dark. And Mick?"

"Yeah?"

"We're fifty-fifty now." As soon as I said it, as soon as the words left my mouth, I realized I meant it. I wasn't playing games. I was eager. Genuinely excited. Ready to get back out there and make some serious dough.

"Sixty-forty," he said as he casually poured a cup of lukewarm coffee. Any faint hint of weakness I'd momentarily witnessed in him (or maybe imagined) was gone. "Don't push it, punk," he said, giving me a little wink as he put his lips to the mug.

AUTHOR'S NOTE

Stories in this collection first appeared, in slightly different format, in the following publications.

"Frank's Beach" and "Jim Limey's Confession" in *Ellery Queen Mystery Magazine.*

"Pleasant Grove" in *Floyd County Moonshine* and republished in *Best American Mystery Stories 2014.*

"Shooting Creek" and "That Time" in *Thuglit.*

"The Pawn" in *Prime Number Magazine.*

"Moss Man" *in The Ghost Story.*

"Joyride" in *All Due Respect.*

ACKNOWLEDGMENTS

It takes a village to create a book, and I have many to thank for this one. Every writer needs a first reader they can trust. For me, that person is LauraBess Kenny. What initially started as an experiment, eventually turned into a necessity. She's an exceptional reader and line editor, and I value and depend on her input and dedication. To Matthew Vollmer, who can dive into a story and trim the fat in almost magical fashion. He's helped me grow as a writer and pushed me to take chances I would've never considered earlier in my career. To my son, Mason, who has a keen eye for details and took the cover shot. And also to Danielle Buynak who did a great job with the cover design. To the Camargo Foundation in Cassis, France, for giving me the time and space to work on some of the stories included in this collection. The same goes for the Virginia Center for the Creative Arts. I'd like to thank the College of Liberal Arts and Human Sciences at Virginia Tech, and specifically the English Department, for a generous grant that helped fund crucial travel and research. A huge shout-out to Eric Campbell at Down & Out Books, who published this collection and worked tirelessly to get every detail exactly right. Thanks also to Lance Wright at Down & Out for keeping the engine running smoothly and always responding to my many questions with lightning speed.

Much gratitude goes to the following editors who originally published these stories. Janet Hutchings at *Ellery Queen Mystery Magazine*. Aaron Lee Moore at *Floyd County Moonshine*. Otto Penzler and Laura Lippman at *Best American Mystery Stories*. Todd Robinson at *Thuglit*. Cliff Garstang at *Prime Number*. Mike Monson and Chris Rhatigan at *All Due Respect*. Paul Guernsey at *The Ghost Story*.

And thanks go to a handful of others who provided their expertise in various ways. Jean Beasley at the Karen Beasley Sea Turtle Rescue & Rehabilitation Center. Todd Crawford, for talking with me on the beach about all things sea turtle related. Hattie Fletcher, for her insights. To my students, current and former, who often teach me far more than I teach them. Randy Goodenough, for sending me a random article about a man who collected moss in the Pine Barrens. My late Aunt Rena for telling me a story about a man who cleaned outhouses during The Depression. And to my wife, Jocey, for everything else, but mostly for her love and support.

Scott Loring Sanders is the author of two novels, *The Hanging Woods* and *Gray Baby*, as well as a forthcoming collection of essays. His work has been included in *Best American Mystery Stories* and noted in *Best American Essays*. He's a frequent contributor to *Ellery Queen Mystery Magazine* and has also had stories published in *Thuglit, All Due Respect*, and many other crime/mystery publications. His essays have appeared in *Creative Nonfiction, Sweet*, and other literary journals. After living in Virginia for twenty-five years, he now resides in Cambridge, Massachusetts where he teaches Creative Writing at Emerson College and Lesley University.

OTHER TITLES FROM DOWN AND OUT BOOKS

See www.DownAndOutBooks.com for complete list

By J.L. Abramo
Chasing Charlie Chan
Circling the Runway
Brooklyn Justice
Coney Island Avenue (*)

By Trey R. Barker
Exit Blood
Death is Not Forever
No Harder Prison

By Eric Beetner (editor)
Unloaded

By Eric Beetner
and Frank Zafiro
The Backlist
The Shortlist

By G.J. Brown
Falling

By Angel Luis Colón
No Happy Endings
Meat City on Fire (*)

By Shawn Corridan
and Gary Waid
Gitmo (*)

By Frank De Blase
Pine Box for a Pin-Up
Busted Valentines
A Cougar's Kiss

By Les Edgerton
The Genuine, Imitation,
Plastic Kidnapping
Lagniappe (*)
Just Like That (*)

By Danny Gardner
A Negro and an Ofay (*)

By Jack Getze
Big Mojo
Big Shoes
Colonel Maggie & the Black Kachina

By Richard Godwin
Wrong Crowd
Buffalo and Sour Mash
Crystal on Electric Acetate (*)

By Jeffery Hess
Beachhead
Cold War Canoe Club (*)

By Matt Hilton
Rules of Honor
The Lawless Kind
The Devil's Anvil
No Safe Place

By Lawrence Kelter
and Frank Zafiro
The Last Collar

By Lawrence Kelter
Back to Brooklyn (*)

(*)—*Coming Soon*

OTHER TITLES FROM DOWN AND OUT BOOKS

See www.DownAndOutBooks.com for complete list

By Jerry Kennealy
Screen Test
Polo's Long Shot (*)

By Dana King
Worst Enemies
Grind Joint
Resurrection Mall (*)

By Ross Klavan, Tim O'Mara
and Charles Salzberg
Triple Shot

By S.W. Lauden
Crosswise
Crossed Bones (*)

By Paul D. Marks and
Andrew McAleer (editor)
Coast to Coast vol. 1
Coast to Coast vol. 2

By Gerald O'Connor
The Origins of Benjamin Hackett

By Gary Phillips
The Perpetrators
Scoundrels (Editor)
Treacherous
3 the Hard Way

By Thomas Pluck
Bad Boy Boogie (*)

By Tom Pitts
Hustle
American Static (*)

By Robert J. Randisi
Upon My Soul
Souls of the Dead
Envy the Dead

By Charles Salzberg
Devil in the Hole
Swann's Last Song
Swann Dives In
Swann's Way Out

By Scott Loring Sanders
Shooting Creek and Other Stories

By Ryan Sayles
The Subtle Art of Brutality
Warpath
Let Me Put My Stories In You (*)

By John Shepphird
The Shill
Kill the Shill
Beware the Shill

By James R. Tuck (editor)
Mama Tried vol. 1
Mama Tried vol. 2 (*)

By Lono Waiwaiole
Wiley's Lament
Wiley's Shuffle
Wiley's Refrain
Dark Paradise
Leon's Legacy (*)

By Nathan Walpow
The Logan Triad

(*)—Coming Soon

Made in the USA
Lexington, KY
18 January 2018